Secrets
of the
Shingle

Emma Batten

First published in Great Britain by Emma Batten 2016

Printed and bound in the UK

A catalogue record of this book can be found in the British library

ISBN 978-1-9995820-2-9

Edited by Maud Matley

Proof read by Steve Clifford

Cover design by Aaron Birks of Bluebirch Creative from a photo by Emma Batten

www.emmabattenauthor.com

About the Book

This novel is a work of fiction, based in a real places, the main one being a remote, shingle peninsular called Dungeness, on the Kent coast. Within Dungeness only the school, lighthouse, lighthouse keepers' cottages and railway station are based on actual buildings and only the exterior descriptions are accurate.

The settlement, Denge, no longer remains but was formally a very small cluster of fishermen's homes and a pub. It has been deserted since the Second World War and only a memorial stone remains.

I have researched historical details and tried to make the local area as authentic as possible, given the limited amount of information available. Descriptions of the lifeboats are based on the two boats at Dungeness during the period (1894-95). The incident where the lifeboat is called out in icy conditions in February 1895 is based on a true story. The rest of the plot is the product of the author's imagination.

Names and characters are purely fictional; any resemblance to actual persons, living or dead and their homes is purely coincidental.

Please note that any opinions expressed in this novel are those of the fictional characters, not the author.

With many thanks to Maud Matley for her enthusiastic support, proof reading and editing, and to Steve Clifford for his interest in my work and thorough proof-reading. Also thanks Susan Scullino for additional proof reading.

Finally, I would like to thank Michael Golding from Dungeness for his advice and inspirational website: www.dungeness.org.uk

Emma Batten 2018

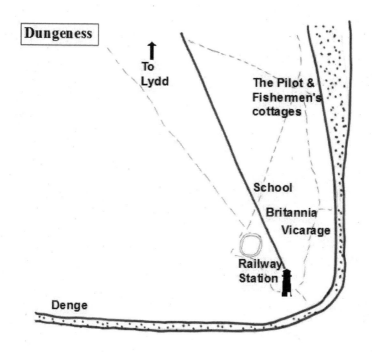

Dungeness

To
Lydd

The Pilot &
Fishermen's
cottages

School

Britannia

Vicarage

Railway
Station

Denge

Chapter One
1894

"Lydd, Lydd. All alight for Lydd. Next stop Dungeness."
The station master called out with all the importance
he could muster. It may only be Lydd, but to him it was
just as important as Paddington or Charing Cross.

Alice peered out of the grimy window as best
she could. The grey drizzle was steady and it seemed
that even though it was just mid-afternoon, dusk was
not far away. There must have been half a dozen
people stepping out onto the platform, pulling hats or
shawls close to them, juggling shopping bags and
scurrying through the red brick station building. A
strong breeze filled the coach as the door was left
open for a few moments and Alice was left with the
taste of soot laden steam in her mouth.

It seemed that no one was going to join them
on this last leg of the journey. It was to be just Alice
and the friendly woman who had been her companion
for the last few miles and whom she now knew to be
wife of the lighthouse keeper. The coach doors had
been slammed shut, the whistle had been blown and
the flag waved when the integrity of the guard, and all
the rules he stood for, were compromised by a
latecomer. A shout alerted the guard, who could not
bring himself to assist this person who disrespected
the Lydd Railway Company timetable, and merely

bristled with annoyance. Then a young man flung himself at the door of the coach, turning the handle and opening the door as the engine made those first slow turns of its great wheels. Belches of steam were being released through the chimney as he staggered into the coach.

"Well, I just saved myself a long walk in this damned miserable weather." His voice was cheerful but rough. Dark blond hair was ragged and there was no sign of a hat to lend him some degree of respectability. Sitting down heavily on a seat, he took a bag from under his thick, grey coat and placed it beside him. On the floor he flung a couple of flat rectangles of wood with leather straps across them. As they slapped upon the floor Alice looked at them with curiosity as her woman companion had a similar pair on the floor beside her.

"Good afternoon to you, Mrs Stevens. Been to see your sister? How is she keeping?" He spoke to the lighthouse keeper's wife.

"Oh, she is very well and I must say the latest baby is bonny."

"Another babe? Well, life in Appledore must suit her, but I'd have liked it better if she had settled for Dungeness."

"I think we both know you would have led her a merry dance, Tom. I'd rather see her married respectably even if she is all the way over in Appledore." Bess Stevens spoke with good humour but it appeared that Alice's first impressions of this man were not unjust.

"We don't often see strangers on the line to Dungeness," Tom remarked, as he gazed at Alice with open curiosity. "And none as pretty as you!"

Alice chose to ignore his bold manner and kept

her eyes firmly lowered. On her left hand she wore a thin gold band with a clear cut glass 'diamond' set in it; proudly she twisted it to and fro. As a nearly-married young woman it was prudent not to encourage the attention of a young man who was clearly in want of manners.

The train had now eased its way out of the station and with a full head of steam it made a steady pace across the bleak land, soon leaving the town and then the fields behind until vast stretches of shingle with gorse and scrub-land stretched as far as Alice could see. They were travelling across the Dungeness peninsular towards the final halt on this track.

"She is our new school mistress and you can treat her with respect Tom Barton, or you'll have the vicar to answer to," Mrs Stevens told him firmly, but the twinkle remained in her eyes and then she turned to Alice, "Miss Tibbs, this is Mr Tom Barton, fisherman at Dungeness. He'll be a neighbour of yours and a little familiar he may be, but he'll keep you well fed."

"Pleased to meet you Mr Barton." Alice raised her eyes to his and the words were forced out politely.

"The pleasure is all mine, Miss Tibbs."

The train was rattling along at a steady pace. Alice strained to see any landmark through both window grime and constant drizzle, so turned her attention yet again to her hands on her lap. She twisted her ring and wondered if Alfred was missing her yet, if he had called in to see her parents after work to enquire if she had left without incident. Would her mother have fussed at his mucky clothes straight from the engine shed and given him one of her lesser quality cups in case he left a trace of oil on the handle?

Still the engine progressed and Alice felt

calmed by the rhythmic sound of the wheels bumping over the joints. After a few minutes the pace eased and the newcomer could just make out the shapes of various buildings scattered in a disorderly fashion not far from the track.

"End of the line for us, Miss Tibbs." Bess Stevens began to gather bags and fasten her shawl. She picked up those slabs of wood and Alice's curiosity was renewed.

Tom Barton stood up as the train came to a stop. He made his way to the door and opened it, stepping out he held it open for the women to pass. Then without pausing to see if any help was needed with bags or cases he was gone, soon vanishing into the misty rain.

Alice knew Dungeness to be remote and looking back she couldn't remember what it was that struck her first about this place. Stepping down she was assaulted by the strong winds bringing the relentless drizzle straight into her face and down her neck. Then there was the smell of the sea that rode on the wind, and the taste of salt and seaweed.

But the landscape – how could it be so changed from all she was used to? How could it be that the orderly streets of Ashford, gardens with neat hedges, flowers and trees were only an hour away by train. Here shingle ridges rode out in all directions, topped with odd unfamiliar plants. The ripples went as far as Alice could see, presumably to the sea which she knew to be there, both because of the smell and because she had been told she was coming to the seaside.

Alice stood for a moment on the station platform and pulled her shawl as tight as she could around her head and shoulders. Through rain laden eyelashes she couldn't quite see the village of Dungeness, but somewhere there must be a small green with neat cottages and, as it was at the seaside, perhaps a row of terraced houses and a promenade. She would see it all if the rain eased tomorrow.

The train had no turntable and slowly began its backwards return to Lydd. Salty rain and soot-infused steam mingled to make an unappetising taste as Alice licked her lips. There was no going back now. Besides, she had a commitment to be here and so this is where she would be for the foreseeable future.

"Were you expecting anyone to meet you?" Mrs Stevens asked. She felt compassion for the young woman who looked quite lost standing there with her smart suitcase and a carpet bag at her feet, slim white hands clutching at her leather handbag. She would be drenched in minutes; that shawl was no match for the fine rain sweeping in from the sea.

"I … err … well I was to go to the vicar." Alice looked around as if there was a vague hope that the comforting figure of a friendly vicar might appear.

"Best come with me then dear, and I'll set you in the right direction."

Bess Stevens slipped her feet into those slabs of wood while Alice wrestled with her shawl. The women stepped off the station platform, not onto a path but onto the shingle and it was now Alice saw the reason for those pieces of wood, which acted as some kind of board, enabling her to move over the shingle without sinking in. With the rain driving straight into her face and the wind making it hard to progress onwards, Alice thought it best to avoid the sight-seeing for that day and to just make do the best she could. So with a case in one hand and carpet bag in the other, she hunched her shoulders, put her head down, fixed her gaze on Mrs Stevens' back and followed the older woman across the shingle.

It must have been ten minutes of slipping and sliding in her neat buttoned-up boots before they paused. All that time the wind had whipped at her shawl and the rain began to seep through her good winter coat at the back. To Alice it seemed as if she was walking through an alien landscape, where the uneven forms of buildings came and went, yet none offered her comfort. No words were exchanged between the two women; the weather and the landscape did not allow it. All their energies were taken by the effort of walking. At last there was some respite from the wind as they stood in the shelter of a wooden building which was not unlike her father's shed at the bottom of the garden, although several times larger.

"The vicar's house," Bess announced. "Just give a tap and go on in. He's a bit deaf, might not hear you in this weather." She was about to turn back towards her own home, it had taken longer than usual to make her way across the shingle with the newcomer in tow and her fire beckoned her, but pity made her pause for a moment. "I'm at the lighthouse keeper's cottage. It's the first stone bungalow with tall chimneys, if you need me. The vicar, he lives here amongst the fishermen, the lighthouse folk live by the lighthouse. We rub along together all right."

Alice murmured her thanks and tapped cautiously on the door of the shed, which was apparently home to the local vicar. When the door was not answered, Alice pressed on the latch, and was thankful the door swung open and she was able to step inside.

At home the front door opened into a hallway with a high ceiling, decorative cornices and a tiled floor which was swept daily and scrubbed regularly. But this was not home, this was some form of shed and the front door led straight into a room. Alice's first impressions were warmth – a very welcome heat coming from a tatty black range – and the yellow glow coming from a couple of lamps. Then she noticed books and papers, lots of them, on the dark wooden shelves stretching from floor to the low plank ceiling and in piles on the side tables and the gate-leg dining table.

There were a couple of easy chairs, upholstered in an olive green velvet and strewn with woollen blankets. It was from under one of these blankets a pair of dark eyes peeped through round, metal rimmed glasses. The figure beneath the blankets looked to be slight and only a small portion of his face showed between the blanket and an off-white night cap.

"Good evening... Miss err..." the vicar raised himself a little in his chair. "I'm sorry my dear, do I know you?"

"Miss Tibbs, Miss Alice Tibbs," the young woman replied with as much confidence as she could muster.

"Tibbs?" A broad smile spread across his face and eyes twinkled. "Now there's a co-incidence, I had a great friend at theological college named Tibbs. Edward Tibbs – ever heard of him?"

"He's my father, Sir," Alice replied.

"Dear God, now that is a surprise!" exclaimed the vicar and standing up he took a step towards her, his hand outstretched.

They shook hands with great exuberance on his part and casting aside a collection of blankets he gestured for Alice to sit on the other easy chair.

"Well, well this is a marvellous surprise. What did you say your name was?"

"Alice, Alice Tibbs." She set herself down on the edge of the chair.

"Ah, of course. Miss Tibbs, I had a great friend at college named Tibbs."

"Yes, my father – Edward Tibbs." Alice was beginning to feel that she was in a comedy act at the theatre. She'd been to see a few shows with Alfred, then back to her parents' home for a sweet sherry in the front parlour.

"Your father... I visited him in Ashford, must have been several years ago. He had a splendid young daughter."

"That must have been me," Alice smiled.

The vicar sat for a few moments looking intently at his visitor before finally admitting, "Yes, yes I suppose it was." Then he frowned and continued with, "but whatever brings such a delightful young woman to Dungeness on this miserable evening?"

What had brought Alice here? She was beginning to wonder herself. This was not at all what she expected and suddenly it all seemed a bit too much to cope with. The shock of discovering the vicarage was a shed, not a fine stone building and the vicar himself was not a portly middle aged man with a wife and an afternoon tea set out on china plates upon a lacy tablecloth. Alice began to shiver as she sat there still in her wet coat, with her shawl folded neatly on her lap.

"Would you mind if I just hung my coat by the range? And my shawl too?"

"Of course my dear, you are soaked through." The vicar stood up and busied himself with arranging a couple of chairs to air the clothes on. "And tea? We must have tea; they say that many of life's problems are helped with a cup of tea, although I prefer a glass of port!"

So Alice found herself sitting back in the chair with a cup of tea beside her and a piece of fruit cake. She still hadn't told the vicar why she was there and he had been so busy fussing over the tea and cake that it seemed to have slipped his mind.

"Sir... I came... it was my father, Edward Tibbs; he suggested that I might be of some use."

"Edward Tibbs – your father!" The vicar leant forwards clapping his hands together. "Well, that is a surprise. I had a letter from him only this week and here you are!"

"Yes, it was all arranged. You were expecting me?"

"Well it seems to have slipped my mind. I find that happens every now and then." The vicar began to search frantically through the pamphlets and papers piled up on his side table. "I'll tell you what we'll do my dear. I'll find that letter and then I'm sure it will all make sense."

Alice saw the thick cream coloured envelope with her father's neat writing on it and part of the vicarage headed notepaper peeping out of the top. For a moment tears threatened as she felt overwhelmed with homesickness. What would they be doing at home now? Would Alfred have popped in straight after his morning's work in the engine sheds or might he have gone home to change and might he still be there with them now? Would the three of them be sat around the table with its deep red, fringed cloth and overlay of lace? Might they be eating scones or rock cakes and sandwiches? Would all the talk be of their

Alice and how they would miss her, but what a great thing she was doing?

After much sighing and nodding, umming and ahhing, the vicar placed the letter on his knee and looked at Alice.

"So here you are and of course it says all about you in the letter. Your father was replying to a letter of mine where I had told of our desperate need of an assistant teacher here in Dungeness, and here you are."

"Here I am," repeated Alice wearily.

"Well, if I said we needed an assistant then I am sure we do and you'll be very welcome."

"I do hope so." Alice looked at the 'diamond' set in the thin gold band and added, "It's just until the summer, until the end of term. I'll be getting married in August."

"Miss Wilkie will be expecting you, perhaps wondering where you have got to, so I had better take you to the school."

"The school? Would someone be there on a Saturday?"

"Where else would Miss Wilkie be on a miserable day like this? She'll be polishing the slates or whatever the good woman does in her spare time. There will be a room there for you and a roaring fire. It's a fine building the school house. Very fine for a smart young lady like yourself."

Alice felt a surge of relief through her slim body. She had assumed, in fact her father had assumed, that she was to stay with the vicar. Now she learned that she was to set off into the wind and rain again, but to the school house. The very name told of respectability and the vicar himself had said that it was a fine building.

Alice took her teacup and plate to the sink, then began to put on her coat and as she buttoned it up she was pleased to find that it wasn't too damp. Her shawl had dried out nicely too and she gathered it tight around her head and neck, knowing that the wind would do its best to whip it out of place. Turning back to the vicar she found him fast asleep, glasses askew and the letter from her father slipping down the blanket towards the wooden floor.

So, rather than disturb him, Alice made the decision to set out alone to find the schoolhouse. She could call in at the lighthouse keeper's cottage to get directions if necessary. Yes, she would ask for directions and then make her way to Miss Wilkie and the schoolhouse.

Chapter Two

Alice stood for a moment with her back to the door of the vicarage-cum-shed. She looked upwards, thankful the rain had eased, and was rewarded by a shaft of light flashing across the dusky sky. With hands gripping her case and carpet bag, she took her first tentative steps across the shingle towards the lighthouse.

There was no visible path, so although Alice's journey to the lighthouse was not far, it was clearly going to be a battle to stay steady on the shingle with the wind pushing at her side. Sure of a welcome and good advice from Mrs Stevens, the young teacher felt renewed optimism that she would soon be on her way to the order and comfort of the schoolhouse.

Dusk was rapidly giving way to night and as Alice felt compelled to look at the guiding light which flashed every few seconds, it made it harder for her eyes to adjust in order to take in her surroundings. There were a few homes, if that was what they were, between the young woman and the lighthouse. Small, low and irregular, there was the hint of light behind heavily curtained windows and the whiff of a driftwood fire in the air. The shacks were scattered at random and as for the streets, there seemed to be none. Alice could see nothing substantial enough to be a schoolhouse, but when the vicarage was a shed, she felt incapable of imagining what a Dungeness schoolhouse would look like.

Another flash of yellow-white and, temporarily blinded, Alice caught her foot on a piece of rope or perhaps a trailing plant. A dip in the shingle threw her doubly off balance and she landed heavily on her right knee and elbow. She lay for a moment, nervous that movement would cause a sharp pain, before tentatively sitting up. The sharp smack of stone on her slim body had caused temporary pain to rip through her, but it subsided and Alice felt that she would suffer no more than uncomfortable bruising.

Reaching out to pick up the case and carpet bag, Alice prepared to push herself up from her shingle seat. It was then that the lighthouse beam flashed again and for just a split second Alice saw another figure on the shingle, just feet away from where she had fallen. This figure – and could she be sure it really was a figure? – was probably what she had tripped over.

Another flash and it was confirmed there definitely was a bundle of rough skirt and coat. Heart thumping so loud that surely it could wake the dead... what an awful thought... not the dead, please not the dead... Alice crawled across the shingle towards the body. With the wind howling as it was and not wanting to go any closer than necessary to the possibly dead body, Alice paused at arm's length and nervously strung together a few inadequate words.

"Hello... I'm... I... Can I help you?"

No response. Alice stretched her arm out and gave the body a small prod, ready to recoil if it rolled to show a pale lifeless face. It didn't roll; it didn't respond at all. Alice shuffled forward a fraction and reached out to touch long hair, matted and thick with salt water. So, this woman had come from the sea;

perhaps the wife of a fisherman. Did fishermen take their wives to sea?

There was a groan? Or was there? How could the faintest of groans be distinguished from the whistle of the wind and the creaking of the wooden shacks? Then a slight movement of the body. Relief flooded through Alice and her chest ceased to hurt quite so much from her pounding heart. Alice leant forwards to find an ear under the tangled heap of hair.

"Hello, can you hear me?"

Another flash of light and although Alice heard nothing of her weak voice she saw the woman's salt encrusted lips move and her grey eyes fixed on Alice's own brown eyes. The moment passed, but they had made a connection and Alice knew that this stranger was begging for her help. When the light moved across the woman's face again her eyes were closed, dark rings encircled them and shadows settled in the hollows under her cheek bones.

She needed to get help and quickly, that was clear, and warmth... this woman needed to be kept warm so Alice must use her own shawl... that was what must be done. But as she began to remove her shawl a new sound reached her through the relentless howl of the wind. It sounded a bit like the pull of the tide as it drags the shingle back with it and then a thud, a pull on the shingle and then a thud in a rhythmic pattern and possibly coming towards her. As Alice concentrated on this noise, trying to separate it from all the other sounds that the wind created, a shout came, carried on a gust.

Afterwards Alice wondered why she hadn't welcomed that shout and battled through the wind towards its source. But somehow her instincts took over and, without even pausing to fling her shawl over the dying woman, she scrambled over the shingle and to the shelter of a woodpile. From her hiding place Alice peeped through the gaps in the driftwood and had only just got herself in place when the beam of light showed a group of five men hauling a great sack along by ropes. They were well wrapped up with long coats, snug woollen hats and sturdy fishermen's boots. Their hoods were pulled low over their faces and bodies hunched as they took the strain of their load.

When the light shone again, Alice heard a curse and saw one of the men tripping over the body on the shingle and then they were all huddled around the woman, whispering furiously. One man flung her over his shoulder and the group continued on their way.

"She'll be fine now," Alice muttered to herself. "They'll know how to help her." But the tightening of her throat and twist of her stomach, came as a sign that deep down she knew the woman was not safe with these men and whatever they were up to on this stormy evening was something that Alice Tibbs, vicar's daughter, could not even dare to imagine.

Alice waited for about five minutes, crouched behind the driftwood log pile, watching the clouds race across the black sky and the rhythmic shaft of yellow light which became mesmerising as she became stiff and cold. Finally, Alice judged that the men were now some way away, and besides they would never spot her as she continued to the lighthouse. She picked up her suitcase and trudged onwards.

The lighthouse keeper's cottage was one of a pair – a solid, square, stone-built, single story property with a porch to the front and a small window either side. The chimneys were tall and the roof was slate. Alice rapped on the door as hard as she could and was soon rewarded by its being opened a crack and the round face of a boy peeped out. His brown eyes were curious, his hair a mop of brown curls and his face had a smattering of freckles across his nose and cheeks.

"Who is it, Bill?" came the voice of Mrs Stevens from within the cottage.

"I dunno. A woman. She looks posh."

"Well let her in, out of the wind."

The door was opened wider and Alice stepped into the porch and then through to a kitchen. The boy immediately sat back down at the large pine table and stuffed the last of his bread into his mouth. There were four other children, the smallest was a boy of perhaps three years old; he was having his face wiped by a girl who at about eleven must be the oldest of the five. Then another girl of about seven and a boy a little older. All with the wild brown curls of their brother Bill, their freckled faces and brown eyes fixed upon Alice.

"It's Miss Tibbs," Mrs Stevens announced. "Children, it's Miss Tibbs that I was just telling you about." She was pouring tea from a huge old brown teapot into a variety of mismatched cups. "Victoria, another cup for Miss Tibbs," and the flow of the tea continued without disruption.

"I'm sorry, I… I just …."

"No need to explain," Mrs Stevens pulled out a chair and placed the cup of tea in a space between the debris of the just-finished meal. "I was worried the vicar might leave you to fend for yourself. You did the right thing coming here. You shouldn't be out in this weather but we'll have to get you to the schoolhouse and then you'll be settled for the evening."

"Thank you, I didn't know how to…" Alice

fought back tears. "I didn't know the way."

"Of course you didn't dear; how could you? Bill here will show you when you've had your tea and perhaps something to eat?"

Half an hour later and Alice felt so much better with a plate of fried fish, tomatoes and bread inside her. They were a lively bunch of children and mostly kept her thoughts occupied with the moment as they bombarded her with questions about herself and information about themselves. Amongst this young family was their mother, Bess Stevens, giving orders, breaking up squabbles, soothing the younger ones and at the same time cooking and tidying away. What a contrast to the refrained dignity of supper at home!

"Well, poor Miss Tibbs, you must be so tired, coming all this way and not having a proper welcome," Mrs Stevens began.

"Oh, no... not at all... well maybe a little tired but you've made me so welcome."

"I know for certain you were expected at the schoolhouse, so you'll find a bed made up for you, but I feel for you having to walk all that way in this weather, you not being used to the wind."

"It's not far is it?" Alice asked. For all her polite words, the thought of going out again into the night was daunting and she really was exhausted.

"It must be fifteen minutes," replied Bess. "Bill will fix you up with a pair of back-stays and he'll keep you safe."

"I put them outside the porch, Ma."

"Back-stays?" Alice queried.

"Them's bits of wood, you move along on," Bill informed her.

So Alice left the warmth of the lighthouse keeper's

cottage and with her coat buttoned up and shawl wrapped tight she slipped her boots under the leather straps fixed to flat pieces of wood and slid in an awkward manner after her young companion. Bill set off at quite a pace but although Alice could see the reason for using the shingle shoes it seemed it would take a fair bit of practice before she could lift and move her feet over the shingle ridges. For now she constantly stubbed the toe of her 'shoe' and being weighed down by her suitcase on one side meant that she could not distribute her weight evenly. After a few minutes Alice concluded that to stumble along in just her smart buttoned boots would be easier than learning a new skill in her weary state.

Bill cheerfully carried the back-stays for Alice and informed her that in a few minutes they could walk along the railway track and it would be easier. As his teacher and an adult, Alice felt duty bound to question whether this was a safe plan.

"There won't be any more trains now, Miss," Bill spoke with pity. She may be a teacher but Miss Tibbs didn't seem to know much.

They were nearing the railway station; Alice could clearly make out the shape of the small station building and the raised platform. If only she had known the school was next to the station and had just been able to go straight there, to have avoided tea with the vicar and the discovery of the body on the shingle. Why hadn't the school teacher, Miss Wilkie, been there to meet her from the train? To take her in, away from the wind and sea mist, to seat her by a fire and give her tea and cake placed on a table with a lace trimmed cloth.

They stepped onto the rails and Bill explained, "See Miss, nice and smooth, easier to walk on like

24

them pavements in Ashford town."

Alice could see his point and yes for Bill it was easier, in his sturdy boots and with only their back-stays to carry, but for Alice in her smart town shoes and weighed down by her suitcase she couldn't balance on a single track. So, she settled for walking on the wooden sleepers which although mostly covered in pebbles, offered a more even surface than before.

Alice was so tired and so glad of her young guide she was content to just follow, thankful her back was to the wind and she could just plod along without having to think about much at all until they reached the school. They had been on the train track for about five minutes when Alice realised that there were no buildings in sight and they were now some distance from the lighthouse, the shacks and sheds of Dungeness village.

"Why are we walking away from the village?" Alice asked.

"Because the school isn't near the other places, it's on its own," Bill replied.

Alice made no further comment but thought to herself it was all very odd. The school was usually a central part of any village, along with the church, the pub and a few shops. But nothing about Dungeness could be compared to her experience of other villages and small towns. They must have been ten minutes walking along the track before a white painted building loomed to the right. In the moonlight Alice could see it was a reasonable size with several chimneys and irregular in shape, with a many additional rooms built off the main building which must be the schoolroom.

A picket fence surrounded the school and ran alongside the track. Bill paused to open a gate leading directly from the railway line and Alice stepped through.

"This way to the teachers' house," Bill led the way along the shingle path. "I go the other way in the mornings, but this is your way in."

Around the corner and a plain wooden door was set in the white wall. Alice was tired, really tired and nervous about what life would bring over the next few weeks. Her thoughts felt dulled by the events since she had arrived a few hours before. Now it began to dawn slowly upon her that there was no light showing at the schoolhouse windows, not a glimmer between drawn curtains.

The next thing she noticed was that at the door was a carpet bag. It was her bag and she hadn't put it there.

Chapter Three

"There's a bag here, Miss." Bill gave the carpet bag a prod with his toe.

"Yes, it's mine," Alice replied. "I must have left it behind somewhere."

How had she not noticed that she hadn't held it since... she had it when she left the vicar... so, so since she fell on the shingle? That was it, she had gone to look at the body... the woman, and that was when she had left it behind. How could she have done such a thing? Alice prided herself on having everything in order from her neatly arranged toiletries on her dark wooden dressing table to always being on time for church. Miss Alice Tibbs did not go around leaving her belongings just dumped in any old place.

"Nice of someone to bring it here," Bill commented as he opened the schoolhouse door and pushed it open.

"Yes, very kind." Alice said the words but inside her a horror rose up from the pit of her stomach and inside her head it screamed at her that someone knew she had been there. They knew she had been out there in the night and seen the men and their load; they knew she had seen the body.

There was no Miss Wilkie to greet Alice. No Miss Wilkie to fuss over how late she was and how worried she had been and how she must come in out of the night to be warmed by the fire. No Miss Wilkie to

27

say that how wonderful it was that Miss Tibbs had arrived to help her teach the children.

"She's not Miss Wilkie," Bill replied to Alice's confused questioning. "She's Mrs Stubbs now, married Mr Stubbs from Lydd last month. He's a policeman, you know."

"And she lives?"

"In Lydd of course." Bill informed her.

Bill was gone and Alice left in a room that was both kitchen and living room. The room was chilly but thankfully the range was alight and although the Tibbs family had Martha to deal with the business of keeping the range going, Alice had watched her enough times to feel fairly confident she could add a few logs from the basket and warm the room up a little. She quickly closed the heavy brown curtains, making sure that not one bit of the night sky was showing or more importantly that no unseen person could peer in at her.

Then, in a panic, Alice rushed to the outside door and pulled the bolt across, there was another door (perhaps leading to the school room) and that was already bolted. But, there were two more doors and what if... what if the person who brought the carpet bag was already here. She picked up a poker from beside the range and with her heart thumping, fit to explode, she opened one door. A bedroom, unused. She must check under the bed, in the clothes press, in the chest. All fine. And the other room, the same – press, bed (made this time), chest. All clear. Back to the kitchen and a smaller, narrower door led to... the larder. Nothing there. She was safe... for now.

On her return to the bedroom which was to be hers, Alice noticed a lump under the covers. A clay hot bottle to warm her bed. The young woman began to feel a little less tense. Here was a sign that someone had thought of her comfort.

The bedroom was quite respectable. In fact just as good as any room she would expect a schoolmistress to be given in Ashford, or even Canterbury. There was a thick rug on the floor, sturdy dark wooden furniture, a couple of decent landscape paintings and her bed looked comfortable. There seemed to be no gas lighting, but of course Dungeness was very rural and couldn't be expected to have all the modern conveniences.

Alice opened her case and looked at her belongings, then took out her two good blouses, her tweed skirt, the dress she usually wore to church and the black dress with a white collar. She laid them out carefully in the clothes press. There was a cross stitch sampler at home which showed the value of order and tidiness; something Alice would always aspire to. Not today though; she had a feeling the same rules didn't apply here. Everything else was a bit disorderly in the suitcase and bag but for once it would wait until the morning.

The next hour was spent by first exploring the larder and looking in the cupboards. Alice was pleased to note that some fresh bread, milk, butter, bacon, cheese and eggs had been left on the cool slate shelf in the larder. There was tea too, sugar and some dry ingredients for baking. Again, someone had thought of her, presumably the former Miss Wilkie, now Mrs Stubbs of Lydd.

Finally a small pot of tea was made and Alice sat in one of the easy chairs, her shawl around her for warmth, and read a few pages of a book she had bought from home. She soon realised that she might have been reading the words but her mind was distracted by thoughts of shingle ridges, vicars in huts and most of all a body on the stones with tangled hair like a pile of tarred rope and dark-ringed eyes that holding Alice's own brown eyes for a moment and begging for help.

Ever practical, Alice knew there was nothing to be done about it now, but perhaps some enquiries in the morning? She stood up, wanting to physically shake off those invading thoughts and busied herself with filling the range and closing the damper for the night. Then after checking all the doors and windows again, Alice prepared herself for bed.

Alice saw her coming; she came from the doorway and walked slowly towards the bed. She didn't speak and her expression was of nothing... not fear, not friendship and certainly not aggression. Her hair was thick, long and very wavy; the colour was auburn. Her skin was pale. She stood by the bed and waited... just standing there. Terrified of what was to come next, fear rendered Alice immobile, a scream stuck in her throat as she opened her eyes, and gradually the woman faded away. It was just a dream and no wonder after what had happened, but that knowledge didn't stop her heart from slamming against her chest, forcing Alice to crouch in a foetal position as she waited for the pain to ease.

How long had she been asleep? Alice didn't know, she recalled an hour or more of lying there nervous at every sound. Then she had slept until... until this terror. Alone in a house with no other property nearby, how was she ever to find peace when night-time came? She forced thoughts of Albert, her parents and inconsequential things like piano practice and her collection of dried pressed flowers. Anything to make the fear go. Gradually Alice's heart settled and she accepted that it was just a vision and hardly surprising after all had been endured since her arrival.

The dreams returned: A vicar who sang his sermons and preached his hymns, a lighthouse keeper whose light only shone Monday to Friday, Tom Barton from the train walking in his back-stays with a woman... a woman with auburn hair. Time and time again Alice woke, until finally falling into a deep, dreamless sleep for a few hours. When she woke for the final time it was still an hour before dawn.

When weak morning light shone through the gaps in the curtains, Alice got up, gathered her shawl tightly around her shoulders and pulled back the curtains. She wiped at the condensation but it was just repeated on the exterior of the glass in the form of light rain, so the curtains were left to fall back in place.

It was Sunday and so the best blouse with delicate pearl buttons was taken from the clothes press and Alice dressed as quickly as she could. As she brushed her hair neatly into a bun at the nape of her neck, her face in the mirror looked tired, skin dull and eyes nervous. She attempted a smile but it looked false; it was false. A new day and a new start, she told her reflection, but it stared back weary and barely willing to give the day a chance.

Half an hour later, with the damper open and the range glowing, Alice sat at the table and poured her second cup of tea. The fruit loaf found in the larder had been excellent toasted and as the young woman's fatigue lifted as her curiosity about this new life was revitalised.

It seemed the rain had passed when Alice decided it was time to pull back the curtains. Weak sunshine tempted her to take a look outside and she decided not to peep through grimy squares of glass but to go and have a proper look at the place. Her coat had been left in the kitchen-cum-living room for the night and had been thoroughly dried by the heat from the range. It might be sunny, but would still be chilly so with coat on and hat firmly over her ears, Alice stepped out of the front door, scurried along the path and at the picket fence she turned to look back at the school for the first time in daylight.

The young newcomer couldn't help comparing what she saw with what she was used to. Her experience of schools was that they were generally red brick or stone and this building was painted white. It was small, but of course she had expected that, and modern, although not as fashionable in design as the Victorian schools in her home town. The building looked quite respectable though and the main building even had a tiny cupola for the school bell. The roof was slate and several tall, white painted chimneys protruded. Alice hadn't explored the main school yet, but it was clearly in the larger portion of the building. The living accommodation came out from the rear of the school with three extensions jutting out at right angles and each one just the size of a room. The windows were wooden framed with glass in square panes. It was not an impressive or imposing building but Alice felt satisfied with her first impressions.

The countryside was a different matter, in fact to call it countryside was an injustice to all that was lush pasture and rolling hills. No, this was not countryside but some form of grim, bleak scrub-land. A desert of pebbles. Neither was it seaside, because there was no sea to be seen and no sign of it in the immediate area. However, Alice did concede that the coast was nearby; she knew this because the salt could be smelt on the light wind and because she could see the lighthouse in the distance.

There were ridges of shingle as far as Alice could see. She let her eyes follow the railway tracks towards the building that called itself a station and the smattering of shacks that were apparently homes. There, standing proud, was the lighthouse with its stout base that was a ring of cottages attached to it.

Alice saw no beauty in this land; her ideas of beauty in the countryside were fixed and limited to her study of watercolours of country scenes and likenesses of wild-flowers found in the books she had studied in her not so distant youth. The patches of short, coarse grass and woody broom failed to lift her mood and did not compare to cottage gardens or woods of oak and beech. She did not notice the beauty of delicate lichens nestled amongst the grass and stones. Neither did she marvel at the tenacity of the tiny roots that clung on regardless of the lack of earth and the strong winds.

Walking to the other side of the school, Alice saw beyond the building the shingle became less and the greenery more. It remained flat and uninteresting, nothing caught her eye or inspired Alice to explore further and the view was only broken by the very small town of Lydd which could be distinguished by its church tower and cluster of houses.

Here, at the back of the building, Alice found some chickens, six of them all pecking and fussing around in a pen. In a brick outhouse she found a tin of grain and threw a couple of handfuls in their tray. Whilst the chickens were absorbed, she checked their nesting area and retrieved a couple of brown eggs. Raised beds of soil had scrappy pieces of greenery within them. Perhaps it had been some time since

Miss Wilkie had tended the plot in order to produce fresh vegetables for her dinner. Although satisfied with the chickens, there was nothing else to please Alice in this garden of sorts. The kitchen door was still locked from the inside so she made her way back around to the front door.

In the direction of the sea, some movement caught her attention. A bent figure in black scurried along, coat flapping in the breeze. She couldn't be certain and she had only seen him in the confines of his small home but perhaps this was the vicar, and of course he must be coming to see her. Then it became apparent that there was quite a gathering following in his wake; in their greys and browns they blended into the landscape but as the minutes passed the figures became more distinct and Alice became sure that for some reason the vicar was coming with some form of procession.

She stood waiting and as the vicar neared her he stretched out his arm to shake Alice's hand and did so with gusto.

"Ah, Miss..."

"Tibbs, Alice Tibbs."

"Of course, of course," He nodded furiously and, with his thin head and pointed nose, Alice was suddenly reminded of a small bird frantically pecking at a worm. "Miss Tibbs, you arrived at church in good time. Splendid, did you come far?"

Chapter Four

Alice had planned to explore the school next – to look at the variety of books, study the maps and pictures on the walls and to count the desks so as to get a feel for the place. Instead she was ushered in with a dozen others and became a part of the transformation as school became church.

"Desks first," commanded a scrawny woman, her shawl bound around her with a piece of rough twine. She took one side and Alice (following the lead from those about her) took the other and they set it down at the edge of the room. "So, you're the new young school mistress."

"Miss Tibbs," Alice introduced herself, but couldn't hold out her hand to shake as they were on the second desk by then.

"Is there something wrong at the church?" Alice ventured to ask as they moved the fourth desk.

"Wrong?"

"I mean why are we here today? Has there been some… some storm damage… or something?"

"There is no church," replied her companion in surprise. "Only here, the school."

It wasn't polite to question this woman any further and it was becoming clearer that indeed the school was the church. A small teaching platform did very nicely as a pulpit, kneelers were brought from crates and placed in front of the plain wooden chairs.

More people arrived and began to seat themselves.

"Curiouser and curiouser," Alice thought to herself, strangely drawing comfort from the well-known words of her favourite children's book. This might not be Wonderland but Alice was certainly bemused by it all.

Where should she sit? At home it was quite clear that as daughter of the vicar she sat beside her mother at the front and a little to the side. Alice decided on sitting at the side, perhaps four rows back as there were six rows of seats. That left space for any of the important families who perhaps had their own particular seats. The hymn books were in a box at the doorway so she made her way to them, feeling very conscious of being a newcomer and knowing all eyes were on her, although no one had introduced themselves.

As Alice went to pick up the hymn book with its faded brown cover and worn golden lettering another hand firmly held onto the same book. A huge, rough hand with light brown hairs sprouting from it and short, neat but dirty nails. She looked up at the owner of the hand, her own slim, pale hand still clasping one corner.

"Miss Tibbs," Tom Barton's mouth smiled down at her, but his eyes were hard.

"Mr Barton," she replied with a small nod. Why would he deliberately take the book that she was about to use and what was it about those eyes and that smile? As if he knew things... secrets... but she had none to hide.

"Settling in well?" he asked, hand still on the book, challenging her to back down. "It's a lonely place out here. Just the wind for company at night-time... just the wind and your thoughts and dreams."

36

"Oh, I'll manage very well, thank you Mr Barton." Alice replied with bravado lifting her sharp chin high.

"And you have all your luggage with you?" he asked as if with concern. "You wouldn't like to misplace something out here, would you?"

"I... thank you, I have all I need." Her throat was constricted now and Alice didn't think she could squeeze out another word. What did he mean by that? He was just being polite of course... in his own way... that would be it. But someone knew, someone knew she had mislaid her carpet bag.

His hand released the book now and Alice swung around, almost colliding with Bess Stevens.

"My, you look all nerves today, Miss Tibbs, I'm not surprised, stuck out here all on your own. Come and sit with me and the family." They took over half a row of seats – the lighthouse keeper, his wife and family, with Alice Tibbs feeling safe for that moment in the heart of this family group.

There was a piano in the school which did the job as a church organ and voices sang with gusto, although lacking finesse. The sermon was definitely more for Easter-time than autumn and the vicar commented on several occasions that he was sure he had picked up the wrong notebook. But never mind, as long as the Lord's message was heard, he was sure it wouldn't matter. The prayers were lengthy and with many references to keeping the fishermen and lifeboat crew safe, which was entirely appropriate.

After the best part of an hour his gaze alighted on Alice and the vicar paused as if surprised to see a stranger amongst the weather-beaten regulars.

"Ah, and of course... yes indeed we have a newcomer to our flock and most welcome she is." A pause and a nod. "Yes, here she is Miss... Miss ... and of course we pray that she'll be very happy here in Dungeness."

Alice felt her colour rise as she forced a smile. Bess Stevens gave her arm a pat and all faces swivelled, relieved to have the permission to stare openly if only for a few seconds!

Then the congregation rose from their seats, exchanging a few words with each other, buttoning up coats and cramming on hats. Soon just half a dozen were left and they were busy setting the schoolroom to rights, ready for Monday morning. One of those left was Tom Barton, lifting the desks with ease, carrying the heavy box of hymn books and sometimes catching Alice's eye and giving her a look. He knew. Alice knew he knew – about the carpet bag and the body.

"Splendid to see you here," the vicar said as the door was locked behind them. "Did you come far?"

"Oh no, I was just..." Alice looked in the direction of the schoolhouse living quarters.

"Come on Vicar, enough of your jokes. She's the new school mistress. Our Miss Tibbs," Tom Barton smirked.

"Of course, of course." The vicar nodded frantically. "Our Miss Tibbs, it seems that she is one of us already. I knew her father of course."

"Indeed she is," agreed Mr Barton. "Not a day and she knows the secrets of Dungeness and she'll be one of us until the day she dies."

"How lovely to have settled in so well, my dear. But please Mr Barton, don't speak of her parting yet!" With a broad smile and a pat on her arm, the vicar turned his back on Alice and moved along the pebbles in the direction of the coast and his vicarage shed.

Tom Barton didn't catch her eye again. His

boots were pushed into his back-stays and he too placed his feet on the shingle without his boots sinking in. He passed the vicar with ease and soon his broad figure was indistinguishable amongst the other creatures of this wilderness. Alice shivered, suddenly aware of the cool breeze, and made her way back to the teachers' accommodation, firmly closing and bolting the door behind her.

The milk hadn't turned sour yet, so Alice was able to have two cups of tea. Then she decided she couldn't sit in a chair all day and a walk to the sea would do her good. Having decided on a cheese omelette for her midday meal and a third cup of tea, an apple from the fruit bowl completed her meal. She would worry about her evening meal later and ask Mrs Stubbs about where to buy her food.

The case and bag in the bedroom remained partly packed with Alice's belongings. She had paused beside them several times, knowing that she should put everything away in the clothes press, chest of drawers or the shelves but she couldn't quite bring herself to see this as her home. Shirking her duty was not the way Alice had been brought up, but was she really going to be able to stay in this rather odd place? The back-stays were propped up against the white wall of the schoolhouse; Alice picked them up, finding they were not too awkward to carry and might be useful later. Presumably no trains ran on a Sunday, she hadn't seen one that day, so she decided to take young Bill's advice and walk the tracks towards the coast. In her sturdy boots, used for countryside walks, she could balance fairly well and made good progress along the lines.

After five minutes, Alice paused to see that the distance between schoolhouse and station building was about equal. The wind was still brisk and white clouds scurried across a grey sky, but the rain had passed and occasionally weak sunlight passed through gaps in the clouds.

In front of her, shingle ridges stretched in all directions. Alice saw only grey stones with patches of short tough grass and woody broom. She saw no beauty in the subtle shades of white-grey through to charcoal, beige, fawn and taupe. Just stones, stone-shaped stones. She didn't see anything of interest in the textures – rough, smooth, jagged – or the wonders of a broken stone with its centre of a richer, shiner colour. This land of shingle did not captivate the young woman for one moment. She stopped for a while looked and sighed before continuing on her way, balancing on the tracks.

The track stopped just past the tiny station building, which was hardly bigger than a coach and similar in proportion with an arched roof. Alice thought of the great brick built railway buildings in Ashford, but of course she was being ridiculous in making a comparison; there was no need for such grandeur here.

"It's a different place altogether; no point in comparing it," Alice scolded herself out loud. "It's just for a year, so you may as well get used to it. In fact not even a year; I'll be gone by the end of July."

Considering herself told off, Alice scurried on past the end of the track and straight by the lighthouse keepers' cottages. It would have been lovely to be cosseted by the warmth and friendly atmosphere of the Steven's family cottage but Alice hadn't been brought up to call in somewhere uninvited, so she didn't linger. Besides, it was only a few more steps to the sea and she had become quite eager to see it.

There it was: a steely grey, edged with a froth of white as the waves broke on the steep shingle bank over and over. Grey sea. She expected nothing else on this dull, cloudy day. Alice decided not to negotiate the driftwood and seaweed strewn bank as it was high tide and she was likely to slip right to the edge of the waves. There was no need to go any closer.

Here, almost on the point of Dungeness, Alice could see that to the west there was a large bay. It wasn't clear enough to make out any of the features in detail, but the land rose to hills and cliffs in the direction of Hastings. Much closer to the point were half a dozen isolated cottages, but not enough to give Alice any hope that civilization was at hand. Out in the bay a few small fishing boats were making their way to the beach while the tide was still high.

She would have a look to the east and then return to the schoolhouse, Alice decided. It didn't seem to be far but, even with her shingle shoes, the effort of across the stones was exhausting and there was a feeling it was all rather pointless, that nothing else of interest would be revealed.

"What am I doing?" the young woman muttered to herself.

Images of a proper Sunday afternoon slipped into her head. A stroll around the park, or along the river Stour with Albert. Afternoon tea with his mother or her parents. Holding hands and talking about their thoughts for the future; plans for their own home rather than living with one of the sets of parents. It was all so pleasant and normal. In all her nineteen years Alice's life had moved ahead exactly as expected.

"I thought it would be just the same," she spoke out loud again. She pondered on her words for a moment and felt cross with herself for being so foolish.

41

"Well, not quite the same of course... the same type of people... the same... oh, I don't know what I mean."

There it was, she had rounded the point and it was just the same as the other side. Alice felt unreasonably cross about it and she didn't usually suffer from bad moods. She was tired of course after a poor night's sleep and the events following her arrival were still fresh in her mind. Alice felt cheated; she felt that she hadn't known that she would be coming to this... this odd, desolate place. Her legs ached and she still had to go all the way back to the schoolhouse.

The lighthouse was still behind her and another sort of lighthouse type building was there in front, on the shoreline. She supposed it was an interesting shaped place, long and low with a curved roof. Both roof and walls were built of corrugated iron and a stumpy lighthouse-style steeple perched on the top. Also protruding from the roof was a horn, like the end of a huge trumpet. Another day this would have captured her interest, but today she just sneered at yet another oddity in this strange place and marched on by in the best way the shingle would allow her.

Walking back inland, the dispirited young woman passed in between a group of shed-homes. She saw the vicarage to her right. So, was this where she had fallen last night? It was hard to tell but certainly nearby.

What had happened to that bedraggled young woman? She looked barely alive but their eyes had met and Alice knew she had failed her. She should have somehow ensured her safety. At the very least she had a duty to find out if she was alive and safe. Both strangers, they were sisters in this harsh, unforgiving land. Alice, ever sensible, pulled her thoughts up short, realising she was becoming overly dramatic.

"It's the exhaustion and no wonder," she excused herself out loud and then started upon hearing a response to her words.

"Sit and rest a while, Miss."

There were three of them, scruffy fishermen most likely, sitting on a bench at the front of a long low shack. And, damn him, that Mr Barton was one of the three. Look at how he irritated her causing her to... to use such language, if only in her own head.

"Thank you, no, I am enjoying the walk," Alice lied politely.

"Nice afternoon for a walk," the older man agreed. His hair was a shock of white, his ruddy face deep with wrinkles but his eyes shone a clear, bright blue. "But, if you were tired we'd gladly make space for you."

"No, I am perfectly fine," Alice insisted.

"You're the new school teacher," the next man stated. It wasn't a question as news of the young stranger had reached to every weather-beaten corner of the shingle desert. He looked up at Alice and she saw the same bright eyes in a younger face.

"I am," she replied, determined to move on but brought up to be polite.

"Miss Tibbs, she is." Tom Barton announced. "We've already met."

Damn him again; was he to appear everywhere she went? His eyes were on her, compelling her to keep her thoughts to herself and the secrets of the shingle silent.

"Nice to meet you all." The words sounded rude and Alice knew it as she turned her back on them and walked on.

She was exhausted when she finally reached

the schoolhouse.   Longing for a warm drink and something to eat, then perhaps an hour relaxing in the easy chair.

The front door was locked as it had been when Alice left but as she stepped into the kitchen-cum-living area she was stunned to see someone sitting in the easy chair, which had been pulled close to the range so its occupant could make the most of the radiating heat.

Chapter Five

"I won't usually come on a Sunday, but with you being new here I've made an exception today... only the once mind." Her tone was sharp; this was a woman who clearly made all the rules and expected to be obeyed.

"I... err... thank you."

"There's mutton stew in the oven. Fresh bread and milk in the larder." This was accompanied by nods of her head in the general direction of both oven and larder.

"That's very kind," Alice forced a weary smile. "I wasn't expecting."

"No, well you only arrived yesterday. I'm Mrs Webb, you can call me Peggy. I'll come and prepare a midday meal for you and Mrs Stubbs every school-day and the same for you on a Saturday. Sunday, you manage for yourself. That's excepting today of course. I'll bring your milk, it's goats milk here, and bread too of course." The old woman got up from the armchair and began to gather her coat and wicker basket.

"Lovely, thank you." Alice felt some relief that she would not be totally reliant on her own meagre baking skills.

"I don't gossip. Don't offer advice. I do a job and I go on my way." Her coat was buttoned and she paused to look Alice straight in the eye, "Keep your opinions on what you see to yourself; it's Denge business."

"Denge?" Alice couldn't resist asking.

"Dengemarsh, Dengeness, Dungeness – it's all the same," Peggy replied. "Eyes down. Understood?"

"I see," Alice confirmed. So, she knew too. She knew what Alice had seen.

Mrs Webb, Peggy, made her way to the back door. So that was how she had got in, Alice realised.

"I'll let myself in and out this way," Peggy brandished a key and dropped it into her basket. "And I'll see you tomorrow, you and Mrs Stubbs, or Miss Wilkie as we used to call her."

Alice felt the teapot, it was still warm and even if the leaves were stewed it would do for today. There was time enough to resume normal standards tomorrow!

When Alice woke some time later the room was almost dark. Her first thoughts on waking were of self-disgust as she felt the guilt of an illicit afternoon nap. She spent no time wallowing in the comfort of the old chair or savouring the heat of the range, instead leaping up to busy herself with lighting a couple of oil lamps.

"It doesn't matter... it's to be expected after last night... and the walk too..." Alice was quick to excuse herself and spoke out loud as she briskly pulled the curtains. "It's not as if anyone saw," she added and then as an afterthought, "not that it makes it acceptable, under normal circumstances."

The mutton smelt appetising and Alice realised that she was ravenous. She carefully removed the cooking pot from the oven in the range and spooned the contents onto a plate. Bread and butter from the larder completed the meal. As she sat down Alice thanked God for her meal and began to eat.

Later, having checked that the windows were secure and all three outer doors were locked and bolted – she thought of the door to the school room as an outer door – Alice prepared for bed. She found the warmth of the clay hot water bottle and was grateful to sink into the comfort of her bed. Sleep came quickly.

Not a murmur came from her pale lips but it was her soundless presence that woke Alice. She stood in the corner, silent and still, grey eyes unblinking, auburn hair dulled by the darkness. Heart pounding so much that surely her ribs would crack under the strain, Alice cowered under her blankets; there was nowhere to run. Still the woman's eyes fixed on the young woman in her bed and slowly she faded away. She had meant no harm, but was a reminder of the failure of one stranger to help another.

Pulling a blanket around her shoulders, Alice stumbled out of bed and to the kitchen table where she lit the oil lamp. She placed it on the chest a safe distance from the wall. Now, when she woke in the night she could immediately see there was no threat from anyone. The light would stop her confusion at the time where dreams and reality become slurred.

Alice thought of Alfred and pictured the home that they might choose together. She thought of sitting in front of the bandstand on a Sunday afternoon or walking hand in hand along the pavements of Ashford. Sleep was surprisingly dreamless and when Alice woke there was weak sunlight forcing its way around the gaps in the curtains and through the patches of thinning material.

When a brisk rap announced Mrs Stubbs' arrival the

next morning, Alice's first thought was that the headteacher had come earlier than she would have expected and her second was Mrs Stubbs was clearly a person in possession of good manners as she had knocked on the door. Knocking on the door was of course normal behaviour but in less than forty-eight hours the young woman had come to expect her neighbours to behave not quite as she would expect.

"Miss Tibbs, I am Mrs Stubbs." The teacher removed her coat and hat, placing them on the wooden pegs on the wall. "A pleasure to have you here."

"Thank you." Alice had risen from her chair and sat down again. "I wasn't expecting... I mean not that... would you... would you like a cup of tea?" Alice looked towards the pot and started to get up again, to reach for a cup from the dresser.

Mrs Stubbs was older than Alice had expected. Not that it mattered, it didn't matter at all and Alice hadn't really had the time to consider what Mrs Stubbs would be like. But, now here she was, sitting at the table and Alice was surprised that the newly-wed Mrs Stubbs was not in her early twenties but was perhaps forty or so.

She was dressed just like Alice, in the unofficial uniform of a school teacher: a long black dress, with pleats and a row of small black buttons down the front and a white collar. Her hair, was almost black and streaked with grey, tied back in a knot at the nape of her neck. Alice's own brown hair had been brushed back into a neat bun which shone like a newly fallen conker. Mrs Stubbs was a little taller than Alice and had a very slim figure, her back was straight and she held herself as if she was a person of some importance. As schoolteacher and policeman's wife, she looked just the part.

"Thank you, Miss Tibbs, tea would be perfect," Mrs Stubbs smiled across at her new colleague and liked what she saw. "If I am a little earlier than you expected it is because I have to come by train from Lydd and have no choice but to take the one leaving at half past seven. I think myself lucky though, as the driver makes an exception and allows me to step off here at the school."

"I heard the train," Alice was pouring the tea. Her bacon was in danger of becoming overcooked and she glanced towards it nervously, "Have you eaten?"

"I'll eat here with you before morning school, but I'll see to myself; it was my home for many years before I married." Mrs Stubbs stirred a spoonful of sugar into her tea. "You've met Peggy, I presume, she'll come along mid-morning and prepare our lunch."

"I've met, Mrs Webb, Peggy," Alice confirmed. "She was here yesterday when I returned from a walk."

"And how are you finding Dungeness? A little different from Ashford I know." Her voice was brisk and offered no chance for confidences.

"Very different," Alice agreed. "I'll become used to it though," she spoke the words but didn't for a second believe them.

"Of course you will," Mrs Stubbs agreed. "Now, we'll usually go through to the schoolroom at half past eight and prepare for the children at nine, but today we'll go as soon as you are ready. You'll need to be a quick learner as you are on your own from half past two until the children leave at four."

"On my own?" Alice repeated in alarm.

"I am at the mercy of the steam trains, dear

Miss Tibbs, unless I care to walk miles across the shingle back to Mr Stubbs. The last train leaves at half past two. Besides, I am the exception in being a married teacher; at the very least I must be home to prepare an evening meal for Mr Stubbs."

"Of course." Alice pondered on the unusual situation Mrs Stubbs was in, as it was true she had never known a married female teacher.

"His widowed sister lives with us," Mrs Stubbs explained. "It's a long-standing arrangement and no reason to make any changes on our marriage. She does the domestic chores during the day and I help prepare the evening meal. It suits us all."

"How many pupils are there?" Alice asked, understandably concerned about the time she would be in sole charge.

"I have thirty-two at the moment, their ages are from five years to eleven. Then, I have Ruth and Hazel who help me; they are fifteen and seventeen years old respectively. Ruth comes from the lighthouse, her father is a keeper there. Hazel, is from one of the fishing families, but I have found her to be pleasant and reliable. You'll find them to be a great support."

Alice pondered on what she had learnt. It was not uncommon for a school to have sixty children in a class, not that she had expected it in this remote place. Her own school-days were not that far off and she saw in Mrs Stubbs a woman who was well organised and Alice was sure that with the headteacher, herself and the two older girls, the school would run like clockwork.

Soon the door between schoolhouse and school room was being unbolted and the teachers stepped through, ready to start the day.

They stood at the rear of the school room, with

four rows of double desks in front of them, five desks in each row. Mrs Stubbs immediately started adjusting the desks slightly, muttering about them never being quite right after the disruption of the Sunday church service. A curtain covered the east window, altar and altar rail with only the pulpit there as a reminder the school became a church. However, the pulpit was now the place for Mrs Stubbs to stand high looking down upon her pupils.

"Miss Tibbs, I see your role as keeping a close eye on the youngest pupils, those who sit on the first two rows of desks. If you could place slates and slate pens on the desks, please."

The head teacher pointed in the direction of the long, low shelves running the length of a wall, only pausing for the two entrances into the school. One for the boys and one for the girls. Alice pondered on the reasoning for two doors when both boys and girls were taught together. In her own school the boys and girls had been taught separately with classes for infants, upper infants and juniors.

She lifted a pile of slates and set them neatly on the desks then returned for the slate pens. Mrs Stubbs placed copy books, ink and dip pens on the desks for the older children.

"If you could help me with the sand trays, Miss Tibbs, we'll place them over there."

They carried shallow sand-filled trays and placed them on the floor. Alice remembered her own early school days when letters were traced by her fingers in the sand before she progressed to a slate.

"It's all about repetition of course," stated Mrs Stubbs. "Most of these children have little need for any more than being able to sign their name and perhaps keep a record of the amount of fish caught."

"We have to try our best for them," Alice firmly believed that all children should have the opportunity to learn in school. There would always be one or two pupils who had aspirations to study further, perhaps become a teacher themselves or a clerk. Alice saw it as her duty to encourage all pupils to do their very best, whether they were rich or poor.

"Indeed, but most will have little use for it," Mrs Stubbs said with pessimism.

Alice's mind was still on the time she would be in charge of the school, "What will I do in the afternoon once you have left?"

"Nature study, drill, singing, reading and all with help from Ruth and Hazel. You'll soon become used to our routines and we can discuss it during our lunch break. The rest of it you will find familiar from your own school days and you'll learn as the days progress." Mrs Stubbs' reply was brisk as she began to pull a huge blackboard in a wooden frame to the front of the altar curtain. "Miss Tibbs, I suggest that while I start on today's copy writing, you familiarise yourself with our modest selection of learning tools."

"Of course," Alice went to the old pine shelves and explored the familiar trays of weights and measures, bibles and story books, pens, paintbrushes, papers and inks. None of it any different from those she had used in her own school-days. On the wall hung a vast map showing the great British Empire – from her own small country to the frozen lands of Canada in the north and the sun-baked countries of South Africa, India and Australia. It fascinated Alice that her own Queen was Queen of so much of the world. There she was, the very same print of Queen Victoria that had hung proudly in Alice's classroom when she was a junior. The other prints showed religious scenes.

Alice moved across the room to study an area of the pupils' own work. Neatly drawn and painted images of the grasses, broom and gorse found in the area around the school were displayed on thick, rough paper. Shells and small creatures from both land and sea had also inspired the children. On a wooden plaque, in the centre of the pupils' work the school motto was displayed: 'Play the Game'. Alice pondered on this for a moment.

As Alice admired the detail in some of the pictures she became aware of the scattering of shingle and the voices of children as they scurried towards the school. They came in a trail, like ants, and as they passed through the gate in the picket fence, they turned to the right and went around past the altar end of the building and into their play area.

Mrs Stubbs kept a close eye on the clock and at exactly nine o'clock she opened the girls' door and rang the school bell. Two young women, whom Alice presumed must be Ruth and Hazel each stood by a doorway and the children lined up in two neat lines, boys and girls, from the smallest to the tallest. When the lines were silent Mrs Stubbs gave a nod, Alice opened the boys' door and the pupils were ushered in by the assistants.

They moved to their desks, with girls the furthest from the doorways and boys nearest. Alice recognised Bill Stevens and his sister Victoria, who both gave her shy smiles. She searched for brown curls and freckled faces amongst the younger children and picked out their younger brother and sister.

Morning register began with Mrs Stubbs reading the names and a 'Good morning, Miss' in return.

"We'll start with a short reading from the bible," Mrs Stubbs began and looking towards Alice, "our new teacher, Miss Tibbs, will read to you today."

So Alice walked towards the pulpit-cum-teaching platform and took the place of the headteacher. Standing tall and taking care not to rush, Alice read the passage slowly and clearly. Her first task as a new teacher had begun.

On their return from lunch, the pupils again lined up and this time it was Alice who welcomed them back into school. They settled at their desks and Mrs Stubbs had just started the afternoon register when the boys' door was flung open and shut with a crash.

"'Ere, Miss you'll never believe... you'll never believe what me Ma... what she found on the beach this morning..." Young Fred's breath was ragged and his cheeks pink from exertion.

As the whole class turned to Fred in anticipation, Mrs Stubbs visibly grew an inch and her lips were drawn in as a sign of extreme disapproval.

"Fred, you will leave the room now, knock on the door and enter quietly." The headteacher spoke slowly and firmly. "There is no excuse for being late and no reason ever to speak without raising your hand at the appropriate time."

The whole class slumped in disappointment. Fred did as he was told but on his return to his desk he sat there with his cheeks still rosy and his eyes darting around the room.

"Fred," Mrs Stubbs read his name from the register.

Fred flung his arm in the air and without being given permission to speak the words burst free: "It were a body, right there on the shingle."

There was a gasp from the class. Alice felt the skin on her throat tighten and simultaneously her mouth went dry. Another one, another body just lying there to be found on the beach... or was it another? Could it be? Yes, of course it could be the very same one, just casually discarded, or another new body... Alice's heart began to pound at an uncomfortable pace and she leant for support, just very slightly, against the bookshelf. What type of place had she come to where bodies lay strewn upon the shingle?

Mrs Stubbs was not to be deterred and she showed no sign of either curiosity or concern. Her position as upholder of discipline and order was clear for all to see.

"Frederick Brown, go to the corner and stand in silence."

Fred's step was jaunty as he moved to the back corner. His moment to tell would come and all the time he stood with his back to the class he could relive the story, perhaps adding in a few details. Yes, by the time school ended and his peers were crowding around him, the story would be all the better for having waited another couple of hours.

"Now, this afternoon we'll be drawing with charcoal, taking special care with the shading by rubbing gently with our finger tips. You may go outside and find a stone that has an interesting shape or texture and bring it in to draw."

And so the afternoon continued in an orderly way, just as Mrs Stubbs intended. All the pupils, excepting Fred, had chosen their stones and were absorbed with the task. Ruth read to the youngest ones as they worked.

"Continue with this task until three o'clock and then some singing for about forty minutes." The instructions were given briskly once the steam train was heard passing the school on its journey down to Dungeness station. Mrs Stubbs gave a nod and raised her voice to the class: "Good afternoon boys and girls. Good afternoon Miss Tibbs, Hazel and Ruth." She left through the rear door to the living quarters and then an outer door was heard closing. Alice imagined the headteacher scurrying across to the track as the train could be heard on its return.

The artwork was finished and stacked on the shelves. Alice was aware Frederick (now slumped) had been in the corner for an hour and she had been given no instructions about how long he was expected to remain there. She was now teacher-in-charge and decided to approach the boy.

"Fred."

The boy looked up at her with hope in his brown eyes. "Yes Miss."

"You may sit back at your desk now and join in with the singing."

"Thank you Miss." Fred didn't move but looked intently at Alice. "It were true Miss, what I said."

Alice had never considered to doubt him and now she felt able to ask: "Was it a man or a woman?"

"A woman, Miss, it were a woman, dead on the beach," Fred's voice was low, his gaze unwavering.

"I shall pray for her soul," Alice replied calmly whilst her stomach twisted with the horror of it all.

"That's very kind, Miss Tibbs." Fred turned away and strolled back to his desk.

Alice moved towards the piano, thankful her mother had insisted on daily practice, and she was able to play 'All Things Bright and Beautiful' whilst concentrating very little on either the tune or the children's singing. She was just vaguely aware the piano was badly out of tune.

It was equally fortunate 'Black Beauty' had been a great favourite when Alice was younger and she could read the words whilst her mind was on other matters. The woman found on the shingle absorbed all her thoughts. Who was she and why was she there? Could she possibly... could she be the same woman that Alice had found only two days before?

Four o'clock came and with it the end of Alice's first day of teaching. As a teacher she felt she had been a success but for the fact that she had shown an interest in Frederick's news, whereas she should have remained unmoved and disinterested as Mrs Stubbs had done. It had gone well, but much as she tried to reflect over a cup of tea, back in the schoolhouse, all Alice could remember was the flushed face of Fred and his announcement of there being a body on the beach.

Chapter Six

Head down, shoulders hunched, Alice slid, in her own unique way, across the shingle. The 'toes' of her back-stays were constantly stubbed and she lacked any form of rhythm. It wasn't yet dark but the sky was turning grey and the sun softening in the sky towards the west.

Curiosity drove her onwards – she just had to know if the body was that of the auburn haired young woman. She hadn't survived and her lifeless body was an inconvenience; they didn't want to explain her presence; she had got in the way of their plans and this way was easier. Or worse... she had survived... for a short time until they put an end to it.

What was she doing there on the beach? This woman with whom she had made a connection when grey eyes looked into brown and wordlessly begged for help. Who were 'they'? Who had scooped her up as if she were nothing? And did 'they' know about Alice? Did they know that Alice has seen the woman and what might they do about it?

She saw no one on her trek from schoolhouse to vicarage. The only sign of life being the smoke coming from the chimneys of the lighthouse keepers' stone cottages and the shacks that the local fishermen lived in. Alice took off her back-stays and leant them against the wooden wall of the vicarage, then tapped on the door before raising the latch.

The heat inside the vicarage-shed was quite unbearable for Alice who had become accustomed to the damp, dusk air. The vicar was seated in his chair, a blanket on his knee and a book in his hands. His metal rimmed glasses were askew and Alice suspected that the vicar had been snoozing rather than reading.

"My dear Miss... Miss?" He rose from the chair and put the book on his side table.

"Miss Tibbs, Sir. Alice Tibbs," Alice reminded him. "We met on Saturday and again at the school, when it was the church, I mean on Sunday when you took the service."

"Ah, yes indeed, how kind of you to visit an old man. Do sit down." He had a broad smile breaking through the deep wrinkles on his face and his eyes sparkled a clear blue. Clearly a visitor was very welcome and Alice suspected that his life was quite lonely. "Some tea? Yes of course you would. I just made a pot ... if you wouldn't mind?"

"Of course not."

Alice took cups and saucers from the dresser and set them on the gate-leg table. The jug of milk was keeping cool on a slab of stone in a cupboard, but Alice still lifted its cloth cover, weighted with a circle of beads, and sniffed to be sure. She felt the teapot and it was hot as he said. Whilst Alice busied herself with chores, the vicar eagerly watched her every move and commented on her progress.

"Now this is very nice, dear, most kind." He sat with the cup cradled in long, thin hands. They were clean and white, Alice reflected, not like those of the fishermen who laboured in all kinds of conditions.

"I came because I heard something rather upsetting at the school today," Alice began. "You recall

59

that I came to be the assistant teacher?"

"Indeed I do," his head nodded furiously. "In fact I had a letter informing me of your arrival and here you are. The letter was from… it was from… well, it will come to me shortly."

"It was from Edward Tibbs," Alice supplied.

"How very clever of you!" The old man marvelled, his eyes full of admiration.

"Not at all," Alice admitted. "He is my father and he arranged for me to be here."

"So, you are Miss Tibbs and your father is Edward Tibbs, such a dear friend. Delightful, absolutely delightful."

Alice had been brought up to be polite and especially respectful to her elders and betters. However, it was clear that this conversation could go on enthralling the vicar until the time he needed a nap, and so she needed to forge onwards with her task.

"It was terribly upsetting at the school this afternoon," Alice put down her tea and tried to fix his gaze, to ensure that her words were not misunderstood. "One of the pupils returned from his lunch-break and reported that a body had been found on the beach." She paused for a moment and her companion's furious nodding assured Alice that her words had been heard. "A woman, a body of a woman… here on the beach."

"Indeed there was, my dear Miss Tibbs. I am so sorry that it caused you upset. Did you know her?"

"Know her?" Alice was momentarily lost for words, seeing the woman with her tangle of salty auburn curls, the pale skin and the grey eyes. "No, I just wondered, that is to say, I wondered if it could be true."

"Sadly, it is."

"And was it someone local? Did she have an accident? Perhaps whilst helping with the fishing?"

Alice knew nothing of fishing, only of the sedentary Sunday-afternoon type in the River Stour. She knew nothing of sea fishing, of hauling the boats back across the shingle and unloading the catch. Were women involved with this kind of work? Surely not, but it hadn't taken long to realise that the laws of Dungeness differed from those of the civilised streets of Ashford.

"Was she local?" The vicar repeated her words. "Oh no my dear, I think not."

"Where could she have come from?" Alice wondered aloud.

"Why, the sea of course."

"The sea?"

"Washed up on the tide, it happens, you know."

But had she just been washed up? He said it as if it happened as a regular occurrence, as if it were perfectly acceptable, which of course it wasn't. For someone to be drowned and washed up on the beach was a horrific, devastating incident. It affected people, turned their lives into disarray as children lost a parent or a husband lost a wife. Alice's thoughts lingered over the enormity of such a loss. Still, the question remained: was this a new body or was it that of the woman who had lain on the shingle just two evenings before?

"Have there been any other bodies?" Alice asked cautiously, hoping for a clue.

"Any other bodies?" The vicar leaned forward in his chair and stared directly at Alice over the top of his glasses. "My dear girl, do you think that you have come to a place where numerous bodies lie strewn upon the shingle with no thought of dignity?"

61

"I… of course not… of course that isn't the way we behave at all." (Not in Ashford at least). "I was just wondering if..." Alice allowed her voice to trail away.

"Living by the sea, we do have a body from time to time, but no others recently my dear."

"How very sad… I mean to say, how very sad about this young woman." But Alice didn't know if she was a young woman, so she asked, "Was she a young woman?"

"Why my dear Miss Tibbs, bless you for your concern. Why don't you see for yourself? It would be rude not to as you are here?"

"As I am here?" Alice squeaked nervously.

It was only then that she noticed a long low table at the far side of the room, at the furthest point from the range and not within the comfortable circle of easy chairs and book covered tables. The table had something, a body, upon it, covered with a white sheet. At one end (the head, no doubt) was a single candle burning low.

Alice felt horror shimmer through her body, but not the same degree of shock she would have felt just two days before. She was already becoming accustomed to the fact the rules were different here. There was almost an acceptance that the vicar had the body in his living room, and that Alice had drank tea and talked with the vicar whilst the unknown woman lay in her final sleep.

"Yes, indeed. I shall just go and… and perhaps light another candle for her." Alice began to rise from the chair. This was what she came for, although she hadn't expected to find out in this way.

"Perfect, my dear," the vicar approved.

Slowly Alice moved across the room and forced her leaden arms to pull back the cloth. It only took a glance to see that this woman's hair was brown, streaked with grey. She was not the woman of two nights back. Her face was at peace, despite being bruised by her pounding upon the stone beach and having lines showing signs of her mature age. Alice needn't linger, her question had been answered. At least one question had.

A candle was lit and a prayer hastily muttered before Alice turned to retrieve her coat and shawl from the coat stand. She turned back to the vicar who had been sitting quietly all this time, eyes closed as if not wanting to intrude.

"Thank you for your time; she is at peace now."

"Thank you dear, thank you for coming to see us." He began to close his eyes, but then opened them and leaned forwards, looking at Alice with urgency in those blue eyes. "Miss Tibbs?"

"Yes?"

"You work at the school? Here at Dungeness?"

"I do."

"Then I have an important message for you to relay." The old man rose from his chair and took a step forwards. "The headteacher, Miss Wilkie, could you please tell her that the funeral must be tomorrow."

"Tomorrow?"

"Yes, tomorrow. We can't leave her here like this. Tell Miss Wilkie that it will be tomorrow, in the afternoon."

Alice frowned for a moment, but then she understood. "You mean to say that it will be at the school, that the school will become a church?" She thought for a moment and continued, "At what time? Because there are the children of course, we must think of the children."

"I believe the usual is at two o'clock," the vicar

63

informed her. "Morning school only. The children will be pleased!"

"Yes, yes I suppose they will," Alice agreed.

"We learned yesterday, in a somewhat ill-mannered way, that a body was found on the beach."

Mrs Stubbs addressed the class from her headteacher's platform-cum-pulpit. As her words rang out clear for all to hear, the class sat in silence and she was sure of their attention. Even the youngest ones were rapt. Fred had a broad smile on his face and sat with his back straight, his chest puffed out with pride. It was he who had first told the news and it was worth an hour in the corner.

"I have prepared a short prayer which I shall read aloud to you all whilst we reflect on the sad death of this woman:

"Dear Lord, as we sit in the shadow of death, let your light shine on those who mourn for the loss of an unknown woman and for her family and friends who suffer, unknowing of her fate. May we rejoice in your holy comfort and be grateful for the good life you have bestowed upon us. Amen."

The class solemnly repeated 'Amen' and waited in anticipation for Mrs Stubbs' next words. Unlike Alice, they were well versed in the traditions of Dungeness and knew what was coming next:

"Sadly, the school will be used for the funeral service at two o'clock this afternoon. I am sorry to say that school will be closed this afternoon."

Nods and half-grins of approval rippled through her enthralled audience. Fred felt that as yesterday's reporter of the news, his status should not go unforgotten and with no thought other than immediate gratification he piped up with:

"That were my news that gave us a half day, I say we play bat and ball, girls versus boys!"

"Frederick, go to the corner immediately," the headmistress's voice was rich with fury.

Fred bounced along the well-worn track between his desk and the corner of the classroom.

Lunch time brought with it Mrs Webb, and a tasty fish pie, followed by stewed apples and custard.

"Mrs Stubbs brought them apples from her garden in Lydd," Peggy volunteered the information as she dished up the fruit.

"Very nice, what a treat," Alice replied, looking up from her book. She found it a little uncomfortable, just the three of them in the kitchen-cum-living room and followed Mrs Stubbs' lead by picking up a book rather than making conversation.

"You'll take some home, won't you Peggy?" Mrs Stubbs looked towards the wicker basket which she had brought in from home that morning.

"Thank you, Mrs Stubbs, I don't mind if I do." The apples were already snug in the basket, protected by an old cloth.

Alice excused herself and went to her room and it was from her bedroom window she spotted the small funeral procession moving slowly across the undulating shingle ridges. Six stooped men carried the coffin and gathered in a small group behind were another dozen men and women. They were well wrapped up and it wasn't until they entered the gate at the picket fence that Alice saw that most of the mourners were elderly. As the vicar led the group into the school-church, Alice turned away from the window and returned to the kitchen-cum-living room.

"We'll be going through then," Peggy had her

hand on the door leading through to the school. Mrs Stubbs and Alice followed.

"Will you have time?" Alice asked, knowing that the train to Lydd would not wait for the teacher.

"It will be a short service," Mrs Stubbs informed. "With no family or friends and besides she'll have to catch the train to Lydd."

"The train to Lydd?" Alice repeated. She must have misunderstood, the headteacher must be referring to herself as 'she'.

"The dead woman," confirmed Peggy. "We don't bury 'em here in the stones, she'll lie more peaceful in a bit o' earth."

They went through the doorway and into the school; already some of the desks had been moved aside for the small congregation. The unknown woman lay on a long, low table and the other local people were seated. Alice and Mrs Stubbs placed themselves at the back, and Peggy sat next to a man with a forest of hair on his face, who presumably was her husband.

"We are here today to give our respects to this woman whom we found amongst us." The vicar paused and gazed at the small congregation, "The boats have gone out with the tide... I mean to say that many of us cannot be here this afternoon, but their prayers are with us. We know nothing of this woman and of where she came from but we can pray for her soul, nonetheless."

The service was very short and the dead woman made good time for her appointment with the passing train. She was placed unescorted into a luggage van and Mrs Stubbs stepped up into the carriage.

"She'll be met by the vicar of Lydd," his colleague reported. "Now time for a cup of tea I think."

Chapter Seven

Dear Albert,

On writing this letter, I have been here only three days, but already I miss you, Mother, Father and all that is dear to me. It is the silliest things I think of whilst I put pen to paper, such as the ripe fruit on the trees at the end of our garden and the autumnal colours on the trees. You see, it is all so different here, nothing at all like I expected. I have come to the seaside but there is no promenade, such as in Hythe, merely a very steep shingle beach. It is not only the beach that is shingle, the whole area is a mass of pebbles. The schoolhouse is perhaps fifteen minute's walk from the sea, yet it sits on shingle, not earth. I write of walking but there are no pavements and certainly not a road. I have to slip and slide across the stones and am only grateful that I brought my stout walking boots, although I feared they were a little scruffy. There is no greenery here, just rough grass, gorse and broom. It really is the most Godforsaken place (may Father forgive me).

My work is fine and the children pleasant, although I cannot imagine what prospects they have living here. The headteacher is a Mrs Stubbs, newly married and now living in Lydd. She arrives by train daily; it is the only form of civilization I see in this place. I live alone in the schoolhouse and a local woman brings me food and prepares a mid-day meal which is very welcome.

It is a very strange place, but I shall say no more because I would not want to cause undue distress on my account. I shall become accustomed to it, no doubt, and in no time at all we shall be reunited at Christmas when I shall have a two week holiday from work.

With my fondest thoughts, your Alice.

Alice felt comforted having written to Albert. For a time her thoughts were back home and her family a little closer. In just a matter of days surely there would be a reply and she would feel less distance from her loved ones. Now to write to Mother and Father; she would tell them about the vicar and her work in the school, then they could compare letters and discuss them. She fetched a fresh sheet of paper and began.

Later, both letters were carefully folded and sealed in envelopes with a stamp in the corner. She would ask Mrs Stubbs if she could post them in Lydd tomorrow. Alice placed them on the chest in her bedroom.

It was still only half past three and Alice didn't feel inclined to spend the rest of the day sitting like an old woman in front of the range. No, that wouldn't do at all; she would stretch her legs and get some fresh air. It wasn't raining and the wind was slight, so best make use of the fair weather before the winter set in.

Alice checked the back door and the door to the school were locked before closing and locking the front door behind her. She walked along the tracks rather than battle with her back-stays and within ten minutes she was at the railway station. Feeling refreshed, Alice paused to consider which way to go next. She decided to veer to the east of the lighthouse and go towards the fishermen's cottages, some of which sat in clusters of three or four and others alone but none of them far from the sea. Many had towers beside them, a little higher than their roofs. Alice had once been to Hastings and recognised these as sheds to store and dry the nets.

There was quite a gathering of children playing chase or tag. They shouted out in glee or frustration. What freedom they had, Alice pondered, not restricted even by the fence of a park or their own back yard. They had no gardens, at least no fence or hedge to define them, just the beach and the open ridges of shingle.

"Here Miss, hello!" one of the young girls called out.

Alice waved back. As she approached the children a girl of perhaps eight or nine ran over. Her hair was a dark brown and somewhere amongst its curls were the remainder of plaits woven just that morning. She wore a long brown dress with a badly stained white apron over the top. Her eyes showed enthusiasm for life although her skin was already coarse beyond its years. When she spoke her voice was rough:

"Miss Tibbs, let me show you around." Dora stretched her arm out to hold Alice's hand. "I'll show you me house."

Alice smiled down at the little girl; she really was endearing. "That would be lovely, thank you. It's very different to my home you know."

"You came from Ashford," Dora stated. "It's a big place."

"That's right."

"It's not near the sea though?"

"No, it's not."

"Poor you," Dora looked up into Alice's face. "At least you came here."

Dora led Alice past three wooden homes, all different with a ramshackle collection of outhouses beside the main cottage. She gave a commentary about who lived in each one and who they were all related to; the names meant nothing to Alice, so she just smiled and nodded.

"That's the lifeboat over there, up on the shingle an' another one in there," the girl pointed to a building on the last ridge before the sea. "The boat's inside. The other boats went out on the tide, except those old ones that are all broken up and no good now. They'll be back after dark, me dad, me uncle and the others and we'll pull the boats up here."

"Does the lifeboat go out much?" Alice asked.

"It were out Friday night," Dora replied. "Ma twisted her ankle and Grandma had to bind it up."

"Why was your mother out?" Alice asked, "Did she go to see your father off on the lifeboat."

"They launch the boat Miss, the women do." Dora looked at Miss Tibbs with pity – a teacher who knew nothing about life!

"Oh, I see," Alice replied, but she didn't 'see' at all.

"An' that's where Alf and Peggy Webb live; you know she does your cookin'." Another wooden shack, quite small and on its own.

"Very nice," said Alice. How very silly. Nice? They weren't nice at all.

"An' that's the Britannia, back over there. They'll go for a drink when they come in later wiv the fish."

"Oh, a pub. Yes, I see."

"An' there's another pub, a bit further along –

The Pilot. Pa goes there too. See over there Miss, that's my place and my nan, she lives with us now. Pa built a room on the side for her. An' that's Ma over there, she's gone to get water from the pump."

All those homes with all those extra little sheds and extensions. All those places where a body – alive or dead – could be stored and maybe no-one need even know about it. Where a community could hide a secret because strangers rarely passed by.

"Do you get many new people come here, Dora?"

"Oh no Miss, well sometimes they come over from Lydd or Denge way. But no one new excepting …."

"Excepting?" Alice repeated.

Dora looked up into Alice's face, as if she wanted to please. "Excepting you of course Miss Tibbs, cos you're new aren't you?"

Alice smiled down, "Yes, I am."

"Do you want to meet me Ma, Miss?"

"It's going to be dark soon, so I think I had better get back to the school and you can have a little longer with your friends." They turned back towards the group of youngsters. "Say 'good afternoon' to your mother from me and I will meet her properly at church on Sunday. How does that sound?"

"That's lovely, thanks Miss."

It was dusk by the time Alice reached the schoolhouse. She felt invigorated by her walk and cheered talking with Dora. It was fascinating to see the area through the eyes of the girl. For the first time Alice felt that she might just be able to become used to her new life.

She came again that night. Alice knew the auburn-haired woman was there before she opened her eyes. Someone was watching, looking down on her; she could sense it. As Alice's heart began to slam upon her ribs, instinctively she shrank back in the bed, arms tight against her chest, hoping to ease the pain. There was nowhere to go, no place to back into. Then the woman began to fade away.

There had been no malice in the young woman's face, nothing to fear in her grey eyes. She wasn't going to cause harm, so why did she come? Yet she didn't come, didn't stand there really. It was all conjured up the mind of a troubled young woman.

The earlier feelings of acceptance had gone. As her heart calmed and her body relaxed, Alice knew that as long as the sea produced unknown bodies and the fate of the woman remained unsolved she would never settle in this desolate place and the night would continue to bring terrors to her. It was another hour until Alice fell asleep but then she slept soundly and when she woke the time was just past seven o'clock.

A light misty rain came with the following morning. It looked as if it was set to last all day and further dampened Alice's already low spirits as she began her third day teaching at Dungeness. The air in her bedroom was chilly so she opened the door through to the kitchen-cum-living room, hoping warmth from the range would seep through.

"Good morning, Miss Tibbs. Through to the schoolroom already?" Mrs Stubbs stepped into the teachers' accommodation, her cheeks flushed a little after her train journey.

"Yes, I thought I'd get the fire lit and then have my breakfast." Alice tied the strings of a coarse apron. The day before it had been suggested that she took the regular task of sweeping out yesterday's ashes before laying out a new fire. Resentment still simmered in Alice's usually mild demeanour; it was the job for a maid, not a teacher. However, there was no maid, only Peggy and she came mid-morning to prepare lunch.

The chore only took a short time, the worst of it being the dust raised as the ashes were gathered and then tipped into a bucket. Later, they would be used as nutrients on the vegetable plot. Once the fire had taken hold, she put a guard in front of it and returned to share a pot of tea with the headteacher.

"All done for today, Mrs Stubbs," Alice reported with false cheeriness when she returned to the schoolhouse.

On her return to the classroom, Alice discovered the fire still lacked spirit and, had to spend more time tempting it to burn with more vigour. Mrs Stubbs remained with her tea, while Alice took her turn to write on the huge blackboard. On a daily basis one of the teachers wrote useful sayings to both improve the minds and handwriting of the pupils who laboriously copied them. Usually she had some pleasure in creating long loops and lines standing tall. Today it was just words on a board and Alice felt quite defiant in not wanting to ponder on those sayings.

'Least said, soonest mended'
'Say well is good, do well is better'
'The devil makes work for idle hands'

The morning went smoothly but Alice found that like the misty drizzle that lingered, her lethargy would not lift. The windows dripped condensation and damp coats gave off a stale odour from the coat pegs by the

73

doors. With spring still five months away, Alice could see that this was the way it would be for much of the time over the coming months and the image was disheartening.

Lunchtime came and with it a cottage pie made by Peggy. As they finished eating, Alice remembered the letter she had written to Albert and the thought of him replying brightened her up.

"Mrs Stubbs, I wrote a letter to Albert and one for my parents, I don't know if there is a post-box nearby, so I wondered if you would mind posting it in Lydd, if it's no trouble to you."

"No trouble at all, Miss Tibbs, I pass the post office on the way home."

"I have stamps already on them." Alice stood up from the table and went to get the letters from the chest of drawers in her room. They were not on the side where she had put them, perhaps they had slipped off... or had she left them elsewhere?

"I can't seem to find them, it's very odd, I'm sure I put them in my room, but perhaps ...." She looked on the bookshelf in the living room. "No, I definitely put the stamps on and put them safely in my room."

Peggy came back in from giving the vegetable peelings to the chickens and started filling the sink with hot water from the hob.

"What's that you've mislaid, Miss Tibbs?"

"My letter... my letter to Albert and one for my parents too. I just don't understand."

"No need to worry, Miss Tibbs. I've got them right here, ready to put in the post for you." Peggy patted the pocket of her apron.

"You have my letters?"

"Well, they weren't going to get posted stuck

74

there in your room, were they dear? You leave it to Peggy and they'll be on their way as soon as I'm done here. Now, who's for a nice cup of tea?"

With Mrs Stubbs not making any further offer to take them and with Alice unable to snatch them herself she felt powerless to demand her precious letters back. If her bedroom were not private then she would ensure any other letters were put away and she would find a way to post them herself. Alice settled down to read a book but couldn't concentrate as a bitterness settled on her and her thoughts were occupied with the knowledge that her private belongings had been moved.

The day continued with Alice feeling dogged by feelings of depression and general dissatisfaction with her new life. In the afternoon the rain had eased but the clouds lay low above the shingle landscape and when they went outside for drill, neither the lighthouses to the south or Lydd church tower to the north could be seen. After fifteen minutes of 'Black Beauty', Alice's school day had ended and she stood at the front of the school watching the backs of the departing children.

Sitting down with a pot of tea, Alice couldn't shift the feeling that something terrible was about to happen. The curtains had been pulled tight shut and all doors to the school and house had been locked and bolted where possible. The windows were securely shut. There was nothing more to be done but sit and wait.

Chapter Eight

It was about six o'clock when Alice was startled by a frantic banging on her front door. The handle was being turned and the door was shaking. Then, before she had tentatively made her way to the door, it was her bedroom window being rapped and surely a pane of glass would break at any moment. No sooner had the thought crossed her mind, it was followed by the sound of glass cracking under pressure. It was at this point that Alice called out:

"I'm here, come to the door and tell me what you want."

There was nothing to do but face whoever had come across the shingle in the darkness, their anger not abated by the walk. She heard the stamp of boots on the stones as the stranger stormed back to the door.

"Who is it?" Alice called, "There's nothing here of value, it's just the schoolhouse."

"I've come from over Denge way lookin' for my wife and I'll not be givin' up until she's back where she belongs. You're hidin' her, one of you are. So, let me in and I'll have a look for myself."

"I shall not let you in until I can be sure you'll do me no harm," Alice spoke with bravado but her slim body shook with fear. "I don't know of your wife. Why would you think she could be here?"

"This looks like as good a place as any. Out of

the way. You'd think I wouldn't come searchin' all this way. An' as to why she'd be here? Not by her choice, but they've hidden her away somewhere, you can be sure of that." He pushed on the door again, rattling the bolts.

"And if I show you she is not here, will you leave me in peace?"

"I'm not out to cause trouble for them that haven't harmed my Emily."

Alice slid back the bolts and opened the door; he would have broken it down within minutes if hindered any longer. He came in, barging past her and stood by the range, eyes scanning the room for signs of someone else. He was tall and broad, with curly grey-black hair and a wild beard. His clothes were coarse and patched in many places and his boots were like those of a labourer – sturdy with thick soles and frayed, knotted laces.

"It's just me here, as you can see," Alice hid her shaking hands behind her back and held her pointed chin high.

"I'll be lookin' around rather than take your word for it."

"But why... Mr...?"

"Ed... Ed Brooks."

"I'm Miss Tibbs... Alice Tibbs. Why, Mr Brooks, would I have your wife? What would I want her for?"

"You'd not want her for anythin' I'm sure, but they've made you keep her here to teach me a lesson... to teach us a lesson to keep to our own side of the bay. I can see you're not one to make trouble but you got caught up in it maybe." He was beginning to calm down now, seeing Alice was ready to listen.

"You've lost your wife or are you saying she's been taken?"

"Taken, yes that's exactly what I'm sayin'. She's been hidden up somewhere but I'll find my Emily, by God, I will."

He looked at the various doors leading to the school, bedrooms and back outside again. Then stepping towards the school-room door he said, "This goes through to the school, does it? I'll take a look there although I was thinking of a shed or storeroom."

Alice was no longer feeling threatened by the stranger and although she would prefer it if he left peacefully, she could see that if she gave him no trouble he would have a fruitless search and move on into the night. She watched as he looked around the room, checking in large cupboards and especially behind the altar curtain. She said nothing and he searched in silence.

Once back in the schoolhouse, Alice's curiosity got the better of her and she was tempted to ask more about the missing wife:

"Your wife... how long since she... since you last saw her?"

"It were last Friday night, she went out and didn't return."

"And you knew she was coming this way?"

"Oh yes, I know where to come looking. They think I'll keep away but I won't." He moved towards Alice's bedroom door. "I'll just look in here."

Alice felt uncomfortable, to have a man in her bedroom. If Albert were to hear of it... but he wouldn't of course... how very silly... and it wasn't as if this Ed Brooks had been invited. No, she was being polite but he had as good as forced his way in... well that's exactly what he would have done if she hadn't let him in.

"I only came here on Saturday, in the

afternoon," Alice offered the information. "So even if I had seen her, I wouldn't know... I wouldn't know she wasn't from here, would I?"

"You've got a storeroom or an outhouse? She could be there and you'd maybe not even know." He moved to the back door.

"I had a good look, there's the chickens..."

But he had already gone and she heard doors opening and closing, chickens squawking in alarm, logs being pushed aside, then the stamp of his boots on the pebbles as he returned. All she could do was stand and wait.

"There's no sign of her and if you've only been living here a week – and I have no cause to disbelieve you – then you can't be much help to me."

But Alice stood there knowing of two women who had been found in just the few days since her arrival. One she knew to be dead and the other, well she didn't know what had happened to her, other than she looked close to death lying there on the shingle. One she knew was a nameless stranger and the other? Was she known to whoever picked her up as if she was nothing better than an old sack?

Alice knew nothing of this man. Had his wife been fleeing from him? Was that why her eyes had looked so desperate for help? However, if his wife was the dead woman then it was too late to help her and all he could do was visit the newly-dug grave in Lydd.

"There was a woman..."

"I knew it!" Yellowed teeth showed in a snarl of a smile.

"But I don't know... I can't say if it was your Emily."

"You can't, but they can. Those that took her knew what they were doin'. It was my Emily for

79

certain."

"No, they didn't. I'm sure of it. You see..." Alice knew she should tell but she had a feeling that he wasn't ready for the news. "It was a woman's body, brought in by the sea. I'm sorry. She was buried yesterday, Tuesday. They didn't know her name or surely someone would have said."

He paused to consider the news for a moment and then responded with: "No... no, it can't have been my Emily. She swam like a fish and could battle the strongest current. I remember the first time I noticed her, with her hair come all loose, dark red all down her back. She'd been swimming that day." He took a step towards the door, "Thank you, Miss Tibbs, it's not over yet and I'll find her, by God I will. I know she's alive because if she wasn't... I'd feel it here in my heart."

As he stepped through the doorway, Alice called out, "The woman, she had brown hair, going grey. She wasn't your wife."

"No she wasn't," he confirmed, but he hadn't needed to hear it; he was that sure his Emily was still alive.

Now, she had a name, Emily. This young woman with the raggle taggle auburn hair and the grey eyes. She had a husband too, who was desperate to get her back. Alice thought and thought about Emily all evening and she couldn't say (not even to herself) why she hadn't told Ed Brooks what she knew. Perhaps it was because of the temper he had been in and if she told him then he'd be back at the fishermen's cottages, shouting and raging. He would tear them down if he had to, nothing would stop him once he had the scent of Emily in his nostrils. Alice was beginning to know the pupils now and those little ragamuffin children didn't deserve to be terrorised whilst they lay top to tail in their beds.

Emily. The name thundered around in Alice's head and she could find no peace. Her husband had such a temper. Had she chosen to face the desolate shingle-land of Dungeness rather than spend another day with him? Had her eyes begged protection from her husband or from those who picked her up and carted her off? There was no way of knowing.

There was one thing Alice had learnt in her first days here at Dungeness. They had their own laws and set of morals. They would stand together and protect one another, whatever the crime. Alice was sure of it. They whispered their news from fishing boat to wooden shack and there was not a thing that went on that they didn't all know of. They knew Alice had seen the body of Emily Brooks and she feared what it would mean for her.

There was no peace for Alice once she huddled up in bed that night. Dreams were vivid and muddled; Emily with her salted, auburn hair and her eyes that begged for help appeared in them all. Sometimes there was that whisper, a barely audible 'help me' and Alice not knowing whether she was sleeping or awake. Was the whisper in her dreams or did it come from an unsettled ghost?

When morning came, Alice brushed her hair back in a tight coil at the nape of her neck. Looking in the mirror, she saw tired eyes in grey sockets and dull, pale skin. Another night of disturbed sleep. At this rate she would return to Ashford at Christmas having aged a decade in six weeks.

"Good morning, Mrs Stubbs, Miss Tibbs. Nice day innit?" Through the back door came Peggy with a jug of goats' milk and the basket she usually carried.

"Good morning, Peggy," Mrs Stubbs replied. "It's a little earlier than your usual time."

"Well, yes, you are right there Mrs Stubbs, but I had to come and check on our Miss Tibbs, I was that worried about her." Beady eyes turned and looked intently at Alice.

Alice looked down at her tea, "I didn't want to worry you, Mrs Stubbs, there was a bit of a disturbance last night."

"And so, I just came along to see that she hadn't got upset or hurt."

"That's very kind of you Mrs Webb, Peggy. I am absolutely fine; no harm done at all." Alice looked at Peggy directly and continued, "Very kind of you to come all this way to check on me, I do appreciate it." Then turning to Mrs Stubbs: "A Mr Brooks came along, not very late, just after supper, and he was a little distressed as his wife had gone missing. She clearly isn't here, so he went on his way."

"Brooks," Mrs Stubbs paused, frowning as she thought about the name. "It doesn't sound at all familiar. Poor man, what an odd thing to do, to come here looking for his wife. I do hope she wasn't... could she have been the woman who was found on the beach?"

"No, I thought of that," Alice replied, "but he said she had long, red hair and the other woman had brown hair."

"That's good news for him, but it would be good to have given her a name."

"You told him about the dead woman then?" Peggy asked. "You asked if it were his wife did you? Her with the brown hair found washed up by the tide?"

"It wasn't her." Alice turned to her book.

"And did you get talking about any other

bodies?" Peggy persisted.

"Other bodies?" Alice looked up in surprise.

"Did you maybe think that his wife has been washed up before?"

"I merely assured him that the dead woman was not his wife. We spoke of no other dead bodies because he is looking for his wife whom he believes to be alive."

Alice stood up and moved way from the table. She went to her room to tidy her bed and closed the door behind her, although she felt Mrs Webb would have no qualms at all about opening the door and continuing the conversation if she wanted to. A tight knot of anger settled in her chest. Peggy Webb had been sent as a spy from the fishermen's settlement; who was she looking to protect and why?

Leaving her room, Alice shut the door firmly behind her. She had come here to teach and that was her sole purpose, so she marched past the kitchen table and into the schoolroom to prepare for the day ahead.

Chapter Nine

Alice had been invited for afternoon tea and the anticipation brought with it a more positive outlook on her situation. With the low autumn sun leaving a golden light on the stones and the wind barely a whisper, her fatigue had lifted and spirits were high.

It had been after lunch break when Victoria Stevens had approached her "Miss Tibbs, Ma says that maybe you'd like to come back with us after school and stay for your tea. Nothing fancy but she thought maybe you were a bit lonely stuck out here."

So Alice found herself lifting her boots, along with her back-stays, each hand held by a young Stevens, Lilian on her right and George on her left. Bill had gone on ahead with some other boys but Victoria stayed with Alice and the younger children. As they reached the lighthouse keeper's cottage the back-stays were removed and lined up against the wall.

"I keep thinking of you all the way out there in the schoolhouse," Bess Stevens sat down beside Alice at the table. "I just had the feeling that you didn't know what you were coming to and perhaps you are feeling a bit lonely, it being all on its own."

The children were busy with watercolour paints, having devoured cheese scones and teacakes. This was the first chance for Alice to speak freely, without constant interruptions. She liked Mrs Stevens, or Bess as she had been told to call her, and it was good to have the company.

"No, I didn't know what I was coming to," Alice admitted. "I thought it would be a village by the sea, a bit like Hythe but smaller, perhaps with a promenade and some shops..." Her voice trailed off as she pictured the perfect seaside village.

"Oh my dear, it isn't a bit what you expected. It's a bit bleak here and that schoolhouse, there's not a neighbour in sight."

"I just lock the doors and the range keeps me nice and warm." Alice tried to be positive. "And as for being lonely, I have all the children and Mrs Stubbs."

"Well, Mrs Stubbs is a fine woman, but not the type you feel you can have a nice chat with, and come the evening you are a long time on your own. I'm just trying to say that it's bedlam here most of the time but you know where we are if you want to call in for a chat. Just come along after school with Victoria and the others."

"Thank you, I really appreciate it. Perhaps once a week...?"

"That's all arranged then. Another cup of tea?" Bess poured freshly made tea for the two of them and continued, "We had some bother last night, some man from Denge, round the point you know, he came here looking for his wife. Thankfully, William was in and he dealt with him, told him we hadn't seen nor heard of her. They're a rough lot at Denge. Dishonest. You can't trust them if you know what I mean."

"We are meant to have a few pupils from there," Alice told her. "Not that I have seen them. Mrs Stubbs says that they don't appear for weeks at a time. Then maybe they'll come in for a day or two and not be along for another week."

"That sounds about right. Anyway, he was in a

right temper, saying that we had her here. What would we want with someone's wife? It's hard enough to feed our own."

"He came to the schoolhouse, banging on the door in such a temper."

"Oh Lord. Alice, I didn't realise. You really shouldn't be alone out there," Bess shook her head and rested it in her hands. "I just don't know of another way and Mrs Stubbs, well she was there for years with no bother."

"He calmed down when he realised she wasn't there and I was new to the area." Alice tried to reassure her new friend. "He was just so worried, no wonder he was in a state. I do hope he finds her."

"I hope so too, if only to stop him coming round the point and bothering us. Who knows where she went; she could be anywhere."

Alice wondered whether to tell about that first night and what she had seen or rather who she had seen, as it must have been Emily. But however kind and caring Bess was, something stopped Alice from confiding in her. Perhaps next week when she visited it would feel like the right time. Of course Bess knew what it was like to come to Dungeness as a stranger and it would be comforting to exchange experiences. She was about to ask Bess where she had lived before Mr Stevens' work brought him to the lighthouse, when Bill burst in through the door.

"Hello Ma, Miss Tibbs," his cheeks were rosy from running. "Uncle Toby gave me this mackerel for tomorrow. He's just came in and I helped unload the boat."

"No wonder you stink of fish!" His mother laughed, "Best wash your hands before it's everywhere."

"I know Ma." The boy was already at the kitchen sink.

"I'm lucky we get fish most days from Toby," Bess told Alice.

"Your brother?" Alice was unreasonably shocked, "I just presumed that you came here with Mr Stevens… for his work."

"No, I was born over there, where my older brother still lives with his family. My older sister is still here, she married Bert from next door and I went all the way off to the lighthouse! It was only our Rose who moved away; you remember I'd been visiting her in Appledore last Saturday?"

"Yes. Your sister from Appledore. I thought maybe that was where you came from."

"No, Dungeness born and bred I am; it's my William who isn't local. He came all the way from Whitstable. It were a bit of a change for him too."

Dear Albert,

I hope this finds you well. It has only been a few days since my last letter but to write to you gives me a sense of being close by. I find myself in a lonely place. During the day there are the children and Mrs Stubbs, the headteacher, but I also have many hours alone and isolated. I am sure you will think me foolish, so I must explain that the schoolhouse is ten minutes walk from any other property. It sits away from the other homes and I cannot imagine why it was built here. By the time school ends it is almost dusk and with the never-ending winds and misty rain, there is nothing to do but sit and read by the fire or do household chores.

On my first day of teaching a body of a woman was found washed up on the beach. No one knew who she was or where she had come from. On the second day it was a half-day at school so her funeral could be held. I forgot to mention before that there is no church building here and the school is used for the services.

Last night a man came banging at the door and he was searching for his wife. However, it was not the woman who had just been buried. It was another woman gone missing. I couldn't help him so he went on his way. What sort of place have I come to where one woman is dead and another missing, all in less than a week?

My teaching goes well and I find that I have a good rapport with the children. Some of them are very engaging, although they have to be so solemn in school. It is only in the playground or out on a nature walk that I get to see their true personalities.

How I look forward to Christmas-time and two weeks back at home with you, Mother and Father. Please tell them that I shall write soon and I look forwards to letters from you all.

Much love, Alice.

Alice felt soothed for having written; Albert and her parents were only a letter away and once she put pen to paper there was a relief in having shared some of her thoughts. Not all of them though, she couldn't, just couldn't put to paper all that had happened. That would make it too real and feed the guilt that she should have stopped to help poor, desperate Emily.

Now stiff and cold, Alice had been sitting at the table for so long. She stood and rubbed her arms to bring warmth to them and moved to stand by the range. Still not satisfied, she opened the door and added a couple of logs, then moved through to her bedroom to find a stamp to stick on her letter. Alice opened her soft leather pouch in which she kept her good, thick paper and matching envelopes. She reached into a small inner pocket to retrieve a penny lilac; she had brought a dozen of the stamps with her.

The stamps had gone, yet they had been there just two days ago when she had written to both her parents and Albert. She had come into her room, just as she was doing now, taken the stamps out and put them on the letters. Then she had left the letters on her chest of drawers to post later. Had she mistakenly left the stamps on the side, had they slipped down the back? Alice had a thorough search, pulling out the furniture, looking in the drawers, checking and re-checking the leather pouch.

The stamps had gone and all the time she searched she remembered those other letters and Peggy patting the pocket of her apron to show she had them safe. Peggy who had been in her room and pocketed those letters, without permission, but under the pretence of being helpful. Was she being helpful or was she controlling Alice's life?

"You're being unreasonable," Alice muttered to herself. "She's just an old woman, just trying to help."

But the stone that sat heavily in the pit of Alice's stomach told her otherwise. She was trapped here, not just by distance from home. She was stripped of any way of communicating with her family and Albert, reliant on others to send her letters and now to buy her stamps.

Five days. Alice had been at Dungeness for five days. Five days and two bodies. Five days and cut off from any means of communicating with her family. This was enough. No longer would she be timid Alice, yielding to what other people expected of her,

89

dependable and reliable. This place – this grim, miserable place – was going to suck all that was good and moral from her if she didn't leave this very evening.

Never mind how she was going to do it, Alice had to get to Lydd. And in the morning she would be on the way to Appledore and then Ashford. She lay her suitcase open on the bed and started putting her clothes in it, barely folding the smart dresses, skirts and blouses. In the carpet bag went her smart buttoned boots, books and the leather pouch. Then she scoured the living area, picking up her pens, another book and her shawl. The suitcase was put back under her bed and the bag in the clothes press; you never know who might turn up uninvited.

It was too soon to leave; no point in waiting all through the cold damp night at Lydd. Alice sat down with a fresh cup of tea and tried to relax in the easy chair. It wouldn't hurt to have a nap, but she was far too agitated. At eleven o'clock, Alice tipped away the cold tea and washed out the pot and her cup. She took a wedge of fruit cake and wrapped it in brown paper, then a couple of apples that had come from Mrs Stubbs' garden. She put on her coat and wrapped her shawl around herself, then put on her hat and gloves. At the doorstep, Alice pondered for a moment about the key, then stepped back in and put it on the kitchen table and closed the door without locking it.

Chapter Ten

Alice had no choice but to follow the tracks; she knew of no other way. They would take her to Lydd, that was certain, and from there a train to Ashford. She would have to take care to avoid Mrs Stubbs in the town as she made her way, in her upright fashion, to catch the early train. Knowing she should apologise for her failure to stay, yet fearful of doing so, led to a cowardly feeling settling as a tight little knot of guilt in her stomach. The moon slipped in and out from behind the clouds and while Alice welcomed the silver light, it made her fearful of being spotted.

"Who is there to see you?" Alice asked herself aloud. "Who else would be foolish enough to be out here?" She didn't know the answer, whether there were cottages along the track-side or if a farmer might be out at night. She had not ventured in this direction before and there had been no view through the condensation and mist on the day of her arrival.

The sleepers were never clear from a scattering of stones, so not one footstep was taken with ease. At best each step was awkward, at worst she slipped, her fall broken by the case and carpet bag, one in each hand. The case was particularly awkward to carry, making Alice hold one shoulder higher than the other, so it stayed clear of the ground. This lopsided gait caused a nagging pain in her lower back. But the effort and discomfort was nothing to

Alice when every step took her closer to home.

Perhaps an hour had passed when the moon went behind a thick mass of clouds, and as it did so Alice's foot caught on a piece of twisted metal. She came down heavily, her knee hitting the track and her chest coming down hard on her suitcase. Lying sprawled across the track and case for a moment, the pain ripped through her body. Any feelings of exhilaration Alice felt having made her decision to leave were now long gone. They were lost as she battled with every step taken. It was dark, really dark, and cold too. She felt as if she could sleep just there, but the ever sensible part of her said to force herself up and carry on. As Alice's brain told her to move and she willed her body to respond, she suddenly needed to make no effort as she was lifted clear of the tracks and held upright. She didn't even attempt a scream. Perhaps because she knew it was pointless or perhaps because her energy was spent.

It came as no surprise to see her rescuer was Tom Barton. No surprise at all; he seemed to turn up wherever she was and always unwanted. This was no different; she could have managed perfectly well without his assistance.

"So, here I am walking home after visiting my cousin and here you are… in the middle of the night!"

"You seem to make a point of turning up where you are unwanted." Alice's voice was high, "Take your hands off me and I'll be on my way. I'm going home."

"Home is the schoolhouse and as I am going in that direction myself I'll escort you. You'll no doubt slow me down but I can't leave you here like this." Tom's arm remained at her elbow keeping her steady.

"Don't let me hinder you, Mr Barton. I am quite capable of finding my own way." Alice pulled herself free from his grip and found herself floundering on the uneven surface.

"Accept it, Miss Tibbs, you are one of us now." He took her chin for a moment and forced her to look into his face. "You're to come back home and we'll say nothing more of this."

"I'll not come back of my own free will," Alice replied, scowling up at him. "Who are you to tell me what to do?"

Who was he, this Mr Thomas Barton? Just some fisherman who appeared with the sole purpose of belittling her. He was tall and solid, not an ounce of fat on him, just hard muscle from controlling the fishing boat, hauling in the catch, lifting the sodden nets and boxes of fish. At about thirty years old, he was at the peak of his game, experienced but still strong and healthy. He was, no doubt, on the lifeboats too. Brave and willing to go out on a steely grey sea to save lives. Who was he? He was a king around here, someone who had earned respect and was used to doing things his way.

"I've decided to keep an eye on you, make sure you don't get into trouble. Besides, I was one of the local people consulted by Mrs Stubbs and the vicar about employing a second teacher and I don't like to be mistaken."

"I've tried and I just can't stay in this miserable place," Alice's voice rose; she was desperate now to be on her way to Lydd. "Just let me go and you'll find someone more suited. Someone who will put up with all this."

She turned her back on him and took a step towards Lydd, but it took no effort on his part to hold out an arm and take a hold of her suitcase.

"You'll come back, do some teaching and within

93

six months you'll be married to a Dungeness man and thinking nothing of those in Ashford with their fancy ways."

"I'd not marry you," Alice turned back and spat the words at him at him.

"I'd not marry a prissy school teacher!" The moon came out from behind a cloud and she saw he was laughing down at her.

"You said..." She was uncertain. What had he said?

"Not me, but surely someone would have you." He stood back and looked her up and down. "You'll do for someone and then you'll settle down here and keep that pretty little mouth shut."

"How dare you," she screamed back at him. "I'm engaged to be married." Alice brandished the ring as proof. "I will not 'do' for some fisherman or... or... boulderman."

Tom Barton took her hand, looked at the ring and dismissed it. "Where is he now then? Back in Ashford? If you were my woman then you'd be with me."

"I thank God I am not your woman."

Tom lifted her suitcase and started walking along the tracks, back towards Dungeness. Alice paused for a moment, thinking of fleeing without her case, but then bent down to pick up the carpet bag and scurried along, slipping and sliding, whilst he strode along at ease with the stony path.

What was it that he meant by saying she would 'do' for someone? As if she was the only animal left in a market after all the prime stock had sold. And why was it that she wasn't good enough for him? What was he – a fisherman or something – yet too good for her. How dare he call her... what was it?... prissy... well if

94

being prissy meant having good manners then that was just fine. But it wasn't. No, it wasn't fine at all.

They didn't speak for five minutes or so and his temper must have eased as Tom slowed to allow Alice to catch up.

"You have more grit than I thought!" he looked back at her with a half-grin.

"I just want to go home."

"Is our school not good enough? Does it not compare to an Ashford school?"

"It's fine," Alice admitted. "I like it very much."

They walked on, Alice still slipping and sliding but it was easier with him carrying her case. He knew of the body she found on that very first evening. She was sure of it. He knew that she knew. He had found the abandoned carpet bag and left it at the school-house; she was sure of that too.

"What happened to that other woman?" Alice ventured to ask.

"What woman?"

"She was lying on the shingle, near the vicar's cottage. I tripped over her and I thought she was dead, but she wasn't, was she?"

"Keep out of it."

"How can I when I don't know if she is dead or alive? I saw her and I was going to help... she was asking for my help... but I couldn't do anything before she was picked up and carried off." It came out in a rush, all those words that had been left unsaid for a week. "Did she die? She must have done, she haunts me because I didn't save her."

"If she died, she'd have worse enemies to worry about haunting than you, Miss Tibbs." His speed picked up as if to stall her words by making some distance between them.

"She's alive then?" Alice called out.

"We need her alive."

"You need her alive?" Alice repeated.

He didn't reply, just carried on walking, eventually slowing down again and allowing her to catch up and then slowing to her pace. He offered her his arm and stubborn as Alice was, she was also bruised and exhausted, so she took it. When he spoke again, his tone was softer and the subject had been changed:

"I can see it must be lonely for you. You must miss your family and here you are stuck out at the school. You'd be happier with a bit of company, but you've got a decent house there, warm and dry. It didn't seem to bother Miss Wilkie, Mrs Stubbs that is, but it's not for everyone."

Alice appreciated his thoughts and decided to put her curiosity about Emily aside for a moment. "It's only until the end of the summer term, I have my books in the evening and company during the day. If I am to stay then I shall manage."

"You'll stay," he confirmed. "You've had your outburst and now you'll settle down to the teaching."

"I'd just like to be able to write a letter home and to Albert once a week."

"No harm in that if you keep to the weather and how your tapestry is going, or whatever else young ladies like to talk about."

"My stamps have been taken," Alice recoiled at the words. "I mean they are missing."

"I'll have a word with Mrs Webb," he replied, his tone grim.

Again they continued in silence, but this time it was more companionable. Finally as the moon broke free of the clouds and Alice thought that the shingle looked quite beautiful under the soft blue light, they left the tracks and walked to the schoolhouse.

"Do you have the key?" Tom asked.

"I didn't lock it." Alice opened the door. "What's the point? If someone wants to get in here they seem to manage without one."

He put the case on the floor. Alice lit one of the oil lamps and the room looked as if she had never left. A quick look at the clock showed that it was past one o'clock.

As he went to leave Tom turned, "You'll stay now." It was a statement rather than a question.

"Yes, I'll stay."

Alice meant it too. Not because of him and his bullying ways. No, she would stay because the commitment to the children and Mrs Stubbs had been made before she knew what she was coming to. More importantly, she would stay for Emily, to find out what had become of her and release her so she was free to go back around the point to Denge or wherever she had come from. Alice had a reason for staying and with it came renewed energy and determination to solve the mystery of the body found on the shingle.

Chapter Eleven

There were some changes over the next few days. The first happened on the Friday lunchtime when Peggy Webb spoke to Alice, looking directly at her with those beady eyes which saw and knew everything:

"I hear you'd rather keep your own room clean. So, I'll keep to the kitchen and what some people might call communal space in future."

"Thank you Mrs Webb, I have plenty of time to clean my own space," Alice answered, managing to hold her gaze.

Later, after school time, Alice saw that her penny lilacs were on the chest of drawers in her room. She had her stamps but how to send a letter and be sure it would reach its destination? Nonetheless, it was a small victory and Alice felt a shift of power in her favour.

The biggest change was when at the end of that same lunchtime, Hazel returned to the school and announced that she would be moving into the spare bedroom.

"It was Tom Barton that suggested it to Ma," Hazel told Alice. "Here I am all squashed up in that bedroom with my sister's little girls. She's got the baby in with her and Stan. Then there's my brother, Wilf, still at home too and sleeping on the floor. We're all getting under each other's feet and no space for ourselves and here you are with a spare room and maybe getting a bit lonely out here. We'll be company for each other, but I won't get in your way, I'll not be bothering you if you want to write a letter or read a book. I was that excited I ran on ahead to tell you about it. I hope you don't mind, Miss Tibbs… I hope it's all right with you."

"That's marvellous news, Hazel. A wonderful surprise. But do call me Alice, now we are sharing rooms, just Miss Tibbs for the schoolroom."

"Thank you, Miss Tibbs, Alice. Can I look at my room?"

Alice felt pleased with the arrangement. Hazel was a decent young woman and at seventeen years old she was only two years younger than Alice. They would soon become firm friends and the company would certainly be welcome over the winter evenings.

By ten o'clock on the Saturday morning, Hazel had appeared with a bag of clothes in each hand. She enjoyed arranging them in the clothes press and after a cup of tea the young women set out to get more of Hazel's belongings and some bedding from her parents' home.

The light rain of the early morning had passed and the sky was a clear blue with patches of high wispy clouds. The breeze carried a salty reminder that they were by the sea, but not the fishy stench of previous days. Alice was at last walking, in back-stays, with some ease over the pebbles and looking down she saw a soft, understated beauty in the various tones of silver grey, through dove grey to gunmetal, mingled with beige and fawn.

They took the path many of the school children used, leaving the railway track and lighthouse to the right and heading straight to where the fishermen's shacks stood in either small clusters or isolated from their neighbours. As they neared the settlement, children could be seen playing out on the shingle; they waved to Alice and Hazel but let them carry on with their walk. For Alice, there was a great deal of satisfaction to be had from having a purpose for the day. And with the end result being a companion at home.

Hazel's family home was built from rough ship-lap timber, liberally painted in black tar. They approached from the back and Alice noticed a large pen with goats as well as a chicken coop. Timber frames held precious earth, which nurtured hardy winter greens and root vegetables. There were various outbuildings and two additional extensions jutting out from the back of the original rectangular home. Its roof had a low pitch and as they walked around the side to the front Alice saw a ladder leading up to a door in the loft space. To the front it had a large porch facing the beach and, beyond it, the sea. There were two small windows to each side of the porch and Alice found herself appreciating its orderly appearance.

"We normally use the back door, but Ma said to bring you in the front," Hazel said, giving the door a hefty kick to loosen it from the lower frame.

The porch was empty except for a pair of wooden chairs. They stepped through and into the cosy kitchen-cum-living room. This room was very like its counterpart in the Stevens' family home. The range, Belfast sink, scrubbed pine cupboards and shelves ran along the back wall. A large wooden table, with a clutter of teapot, cups, saucers, plates and cutlery in the centre. Easy chairs and a sofa draped with mismatched crocheted blankets gathered around a large rag rug to the left. A dark wooden cabinet with glass doors displayed a collection of fine china and ornaments. To the right was a door that probably led to an inner hallway and the bedrooms.

It was a warm, cosy room and although it lacked the formal style of the Ashford vicarage, Alice was beginning to find a certain charm in unmatched crockery and furniture showing wear from a busy family life. When Hazel's mother offered her a cup of tea and apple cake she was very happy to stay for a while and curious to learn more about the lives of the local families.

"How are you finding your first week teaching, Miss Tibbs?"

"I am liking it very much, Mrs Tanner. I can learn from Mrs Stubbs' experience and it is so worthwhile to be able to teach these young minds." Alice replied politely but her mind was really on how to divert the conversation to the fishing community and the missing Emily.

"Well, it's wonderful for our Hazel to be able to come and live with you. She's been that happy about it. Now, pass Miss Tibbs the sugar, Hazel. Not that I won't miss her, of course I will, but it's got a bit crowded here what with her sister and her three here. Wilf has to sleep in here on the floor." She pointed towards a roll of bedding on the floor. "They are saving up to build a cottage, Annie and Stan I mean, but it will take a while."

"And does Stan fish too?" Alice asked.

"He does, but he goes out in his own boat. They are out on the beach checking over the boats; we don't go fishing on a Saturday but they'll be out a couple of hours before low tide early tomorrow afternoon."

"I saw a smart boat standing high on the beach, is that the lifeboat?" Alice asked.

101

"That's Thomas Simcox," Mrs Tanner told her.

"No, a boat, not a man!" Alice laughed a little to cover her embarrassment.

"I didn't think you'd be talking about any smart young men around here!" Mrs Tanner smiled, "No, Thomas Simcox is the lifeboat and she does look fine up there on the bank. We've had her here, the last two years, she came in '92. Then there's the R.A.O.B, just came this month and she's at the lifeboat station."

"If Alice thinks Thomas Simcox is confusing, she'll never guess what R.A.O.B stands for," Hazel joined in. "Go on have a guess."

"R, maybe Royal … A … O …, I don't know," Alice couldn't imagine, but she felt that this frivolous conversation was doing her good. The tension was easing from her body. "B, well, B for boat?"

"You got one out of four correct, now what do you think of this? Royal Antediluvian Order of the Buffaloes!" Hazel had a big grin on her face, "I can hardly say it myself!"

"Why?"

"It's some charity," Mrs Tanner informed. "They help people in need. This boat – the R.A.O.B – it came on the train, the same as you. My, that were a job to get her brought over the shingle! She's the second one they've given us, the other one were called the same!"

"Well, it's not something I've ever heard of," Alice reflected, "but antediluvian, that means 'before the flood', before Noah's ark, so they must have been around a long time. I'll note it down and when I am back at home for Christmas I'll ask Father if he's heard of it."

"You do that, dear, and then you can come back and tell us all about them."

"I heard the lifeboat was out last weekend," Alice started what she really wanted to talk about.

"She was and I can't help thinking that's where the poor woman came from." Mrs Tanner poured a second cup of tea. "More cake Miss Tibbs?"

"Yes please, it's delicious." Alice pushed her plate forward. "You mean the woman on the beach? The one who was found washed up?"

"Yes, she wasn't from the boat our men went out to because they saved the crew and there were no passengers, but it was rough that night and I hear the Rye boat went out and maybe it didn't go so well."

Hazel had stood and gone to the front window. "It's coming over quite dark, I think we need to get back before the heavens open. I can't believe it was so lovely just an hour ago. Dad and the others will be back in a minute, no need to get wet if they're not at sea."

The young women put their coats on and gathered armfuls of bedding. Hazel strung her smarter boots around her neck and Alice welcomed a basket with goats milk, cheese and cake. They stepped out of the front porch and into their back-stays. Goodbyes were said to Mrs Tanner; Alice assured her that Hazel would be no trouble at all and thanked her for the delicious cake. Hazel promised to visit at least once a week after school and at the weekend.

What a change an hour had made; a mass of dark violet cloud hung over the distant sea, changing it to a steely grey. Looking inland towards Lydd, the day was just as it had been, the clear blue sky not giving a hint of what was to come. The darkening sky over the sea brought with it a change in depth to the colours of the landscape, the greens of the grasses and broom were stronger and the colours of the shingle more

103

pronounced. The young woman moved as quickly as they could, determined to beat the weather.

Hazel's home was one of three in a cluster, but standing alone and slightly inland was another cottage. This one was a natural wood colour with black painted window frames and doors. As they passed by, a woman was outside gathering in the sheets from the washing line. Hazel gave her a wave.

"That's my Aunt Connie,"

The woman waved back and went into the house. There was another woman sitting on a bench by the back door. She was well wrapped up in a blanket or shawl, with only part of her face showing.

"Is that her daughter?" Alice asked.

"Her daughter? No," Hazel replied. "She doesn't have any children. "I heard her husband's cousin was visiting, a distant cousin I presume. I'm not sure but Ma said she was there and not at all well, so we weren't to bother her."

As they looked across, the woman stood up slowly and put her hand out to support herself on the side of the building. She looked towards Alice and Hazel then, as she turned, her shawl slipped away from her head and Alice saw the glint of auburn in her hair. The young woman pulled the shawl around her slim shoulders and stepped into the cottage.

"Are you well, Miss Tibbs… Alice?" Hazel's words broke into her thoughts.

"I… yes. Sorry. I was staring, how very rude. What beautiful hair that young woman had, did you see?"

"A sort of dark copper, yes it was lovely."

"I expect Connie's husband has the same colour, but it's truly lovely on a woman." Alice patted her own chestnut coloured knot of hair. "How pretty hanging in curls down her back; mine is so straight and always back in this sensible knot."

"Perhaps you could let it down, just on a Saturday, do something different?" Hazel suggested. "But of course you want to look proper for teaching and church."

"Yes, I could," Alice said absent-mindedly, because her thoughts were full of the young woman who surely was Emily. "Does Connie's husband have dark copper coloured hair?"

"Oh no, it's straw coloured, like mine, maybe a little darker. No, I don't know of anyone with that colour hair from around here. I think she's come visiting from Hythe way, that's what I heard."

By now the two friends were some way past the fishermen's cottages and the storm clouds were catching up with them. They could see the first heavy drops of rain were falling on the beach and that the men had retreated to their homes or the pub. There was now a sharp chill in the air. Alice and Hazel hurried along, eager to be back home at the schoolhouse.

The next morning, when Alice opened the door between the house and school, she was beginning to feel comfortable with knowing the school would become a church for the next hour. It seemed quite reasonable to make use of a space which would otherwise remain empty on a Sunday. Alice and Hazel stepped through as the first families arrived and started moving the desks to one side and placing extra chairs in rows.

"I knew Ma would be here early," Hazel said as she went over to greet quite a crowd, whom Alice presumed must include her brother, sister and brother-in-law, along with the three children.

Alice wasn't left for long with no one to help her carry a desk, but her partner was not her ideal choice.

"I'm still here; I told you I would be." Alice spoke in a low voice, a scowl on her face.

"I've come to the church, not to check up on you."

"I just thought…"

"There's no need for us to be enemies. I'm looking out for everyone here and doing what's best. We need another teacher, so here you are." Tom Barton made it all sound quite reasonable, picking his end of the desk up with ease and pulling her along in his wake. "Let's call a truce. I've upset you and I'm sorry."

They set down the desk and went for the next one. "Very well, but what about my parents and Albert? I want to write to them or they'll worry." Alice tried to lift her scowl; people were watching.

"You've already written to them."

"One letter was taken from my room without permission and the second was not sent as my stamps had gone missing."

"You can send a letter home, but first I have a little job for you. A chance to show your allegiance to Dungeness and those who live here." Tom looked down at her as they stacked the second desk on top of the first. He must have been a head taller than Alice and his hands were huge with stubby fingers, although she had to admit they were clean with neat nails. He had made an effort for church.

"A job? It sounds like an initiation ceremony. I'm just here for a while; I have no cause to pledge my allegiance. A truce? You just want to push me around as if you are some kind of lord here. Lord of what? A fishing boat and a pile of stones?"

106

Alice turned away, she could move the chairs alone and would not be a part of whatever he was planning. Her body was tense and shaking with anger. From the moment she first saw him, he did nothing but irritate her with his bad manners and domineering ways. There he was, lifting the desks on his own, as if no conversation had taken place between the two of them. As if he could just wait until she came asking for his goodwill and protection.

Afterwards Alice couldn't remember the church service. She could sing along to all the well-known hymns and say the responses whilst all the time her mind was on Emily and the mystery surrounding her. Finally, the vicar gave his parting words, "...and peace be with you." Alice muttered her response and started moving the extra chairs to the side. She made brief comments and nodded politely to the people who introduced themselves as parents to her pupils, whilst having the excuse of still being very new to the school if they thought her a little vague.

Finally, just when she thought she had avoided him, Tom stood between Alice and the doorway through to the house.

"Excuse me, Mr Barton," Alice's voice was cool.

"You'll meet my sister by the station at noon, she'll tell you what needs doing."

"I'll be here preparing my lunch at noon," Alice snapped back at him.

Chapter Twelve

Shoulders rounded and heart heavy, Alice slid alongside the railway tracks. The cloud was low and the breeze carried a sharp chill as swathes of sea-mist rolled inland. Alice's brown woollen hat was pulled low over her ears and her coat buttoned up to her neck. Looking up, she saw the outline of the station and stubbed her back-stay on a stump of broom, causing her rhythmic pace to be lost.

"Damn and blast," she muttered, followed by, "there was no need for that, no need at all."

The young woman waiting in the shelter of the train station gave a brief smile as Alice entered. She was well wrapped up with a tweed coat over a thick woollen dress, and a tasselled shawl covering her head and shoulders. Wisps of curly, dark blonde hair framed her round face and grey eyes looked straight into Alice's own. Under other circumstances, if Alice had met her perhaps at church or in a local shop, she would have liked Thomas Barton's sister on sight.

"We need you to go along to Denge, to give a message to Ed Brooks: tell him that his wife has been ill but we've kept her alive and when he's had a little longer to miss her we'll be ready to talk."

"So you are Mr Barton's sister?" Alice just wanted to be sure.

"I'm Lucie Barton."

"And why me? Why am I being sent with this

message, why not someone who understands why you are holding Mrs Barton?"

"For that very reason, you carry the message but you are no use to them. You know nothing."

So many questions, but clearly no point in asking them; the less she knew the less she could tell. But she did know; Alice knew more than Lucie Barton suspected. Alice knew where Emily was being held and if she told Ed Brooks then maybe he could free her. Or would letting him know of her whereabouts put Emily's life in danger? Alice had already failed Emily once and she had to make the right choices this time. The Reverend Tibbs often advised that if you are not sure what to do then do nothing and wait until God sends you a direction. It was a time to wait.

"How will I find Mr Brooks?"

"I'll walk with you past the lighthouse to the coast and then you'll go on alone, around the point into West Bay and the first settlement you come to is Denge; there is no mistaking it."

Lucie led the way and they moved along in silence for several minutes. Once they reached the point, had the day been clearer Alice could have seen across East Bay to Hythe and Folkestone, then across the west to Rye. Instead, she could barely make out the fishermen's cottages at Dungeness village and their boats on the beach. To the west, the indistinct shapes of shacks and small boats.

"That's Denge. You'll find Ed Brooks easy enough, there's only the two or three families living there."

"And if I run into trouble?"

"We'll come and get you," Lucie said with confidence. "There's not enough of them to stop us."

"Very well."

"You remember the message?" Lucie asked before Alice turned to leave.

"Emily has been ill, but is alive. She is being kept and when he has had longer to miss her, you'll be ready to talk." Alice took her first steps in the direction of Denge.

"Stay along the coast," Lucie called out. "You don't want to get lost in the fog."

Without giving a response, Alice turned and began the trudge along to Denge. There was nothing to see with the clouds closing in all around; the rhythmic blast of the fog trumpet was her only companion. The sea was very close, crashing on the beach and dragging pebbles back in its wake. Ten minutes or so passed and the grey forms of wooden shacks became clearly visible. Denge was no great distance from Dungeness point; yet it seemed to have even less to offer than Dungeness.

The settlement was no more than six low, wooden buildings with an assortment of wood stores, animal shelters and storage sheds. One, a little larger than the others, displayed a crooked sign on its plank wall: *The Hope and Anchor*. A public house. Of course the men would need a place to gather and relax in the evenings. Please may she not have to enter a pub in order to seek out Ed Barton.

The first form of life came to her notice when a mournful sound was carried to Alice on the wafts of mist. A group of nine or ten goats were tethered to strong stakes, short ropes allowed them little freedom and their pitiful bleats told of a lack of fresh greenery. But even after her few days living at Dungeness, Alice recognised the need for fresh milk and clearly this land could not sustain cattle.

Gazing again at the buildings, Alice noted that

each shack had a chimney and wisp of smoke curling upwards. Although it was still early afternoon, curtains were closed tight and some windows were also shuttered. It was as if these Denge creatures had gathered to hibernate over the coming months. There was no way of telling which one Ed Brooks lived in, so Alice rapped on the door of the nearest shack. After a moment it was opened, just an inch or so, and a woman spoke, her tone full of suspicion:

"What do you want?"

"I am looking for Mr Brooks." Alice spoke to the door.

"Well, I don't know what you'd be wantin', comin' out all this way," the door opened a little more and dark eyes in an olive-skinned, shrivelled face looked out. "He lives out the back of us, just step around the back an' his place has got a boarded up window." Alice nodded her thanks. "You'll not be welcome, girl. I'll tell you that much," the old woman called out before closing the door and giving no time for a response.

It really was no better than a garden shed: the one window to the front, not shuttered but boarded up. The ship-lap walls were their natural colour. There was no door knocker, so Alice thumped on the bare wood with her fist.

The door opened and Ed Brooks' black eyes met Alice's own brown ones. The fiery temper had passed and he looked to be a shadow of the man she met just days before. His eyes had dark rings around them, as if he had barely slept in days and, as he stepped back to allow Alice into his home, she saw his body had visibly slumped. If, for some reason, this man had a lesson to be learned then Alice felt it had been done. He was clearly suffering for the loss of his

111

wife.

Once inside the hovel, it took Alice's eyes a moment to adjust as the only light radiated from the fire sitting on a brick hearth, by the end wall to her left. A kettle was slung over a metal hook and a couple of pans hung on the wall. This fire was clearly meant for both cooking and heat. To the left of the chimney breast was a pile of driftwood and logs, to the right was a solid pine cupboard, filling the whole space from floor to the low ceiling.

The one window to the front had been boarded up inside and out, and leaning against it, to the left of Alice as she stood on the threshold, was a selection of tools. A huge fishing net was folded several times and hung from hooks in the ceiling also in front of the window. The two small windows to the rear of the shack had tatty curtains of an unrecognisable colour and pattern.

A tired wooden table and three mismatched chairs stood on the wooden floor in the centre of the room. To Alice's right was a large unmade box bed and a cupboard. Hooks on the rear wall displayed thick coats and a shawl. It was a miserable home, showing few signs that anyone had ever cared to make it a more attractive place to live in.

But worse than any visual assault was the over-riding stench of raw fish and seaweed, coupled with burning wood. Undertones of rotten milk and unwashed body mingled. Alice longed to leave the door open and fling open the rear windows.

"So, you're the school teacher. The new one." He looked into her eyes and she saw no hope left in his.

"I am. They sent me to speak to you."

"Why you? What d'you know?" He turned and

sat on a chair, his upper body supported by the table.

"I know Emily is alive, that she has been very ill but she is alive." Alice remained standing by the doorway; she hadn't been invited to sit and wasn't inclined to.

"I told you she was alive. Tell me somethin' new."

"They are keeping her until you are ready to talk. I'm sorry, that's the message and maybe you know what it means, but I don't."

"I asked why they sent you." Ed reminded Alice.

"Yes, you did. I think because I am a stranger, because I don't know anything so there is nothing I can tell you. I asked them about Emily, but they won't tell me. I know nothing about her, only what they tell me."

"You've not seem her then?"

"I've not seen her," Alice lied.

"I'm ready to talk; I just need her back."

"I'll tell them. But I think it's too soon, that they want you to wait longer."

Ed stood up quickly, causing his chair to fall back onto the floor and Alice to see a glimpse of the man whom she had first met at the schoolhouse.

"Who was it? Who gave you the message?"

"It was a woman; I'd not met her before."

"One of the fishermen's wives?" he barked.

"It must have been."

Ed Brooks turned to right the chair and Alice took the opportunity to leave, closing the door behind her and saying no more. As she scurried away, every step hindered by the uneven surface, she felt sure he would come after her and listened for his heavy steps on the shingle. Alice knew she couldn't stop him and no one here would save her from his fury. The door remained closed though and she moved away from Denge. It would have taken no time at all for him to catch up with her; but for some reason Ed Brooks chose to allow her to leave.

The sea mist was thickening. Alice paused to put on her back-stays and reflected that in the snow they might do nicely as skis. Within a few minutes she had put Denge well behind her and was making good progress.

On nearing the point, Alice had a feeling someone was following her. A scatter of stones and the snapping of a stick, it was nothing that wouldn't be caused by an animal, but Alice feared otherwise. Heart pounding with trepidation, she looked back and was relieved to see a small hunched figure and not the tall, dark threat of Ed Brooks. Alice concentrated on her route over the stones, trying to increase her speed as she was eager to be home but not realising she was being pursued. She was an amateur though and by the time she reached the Point, the figure was almost upon her and Alice looked back to recognise the old hag whose door she had first knocked on when she reached Denge.

"Ain't you going t' stop then?" her voice was rough and her breathing ragged.

"I didn't realise."

"My niece, she's a good hard-working girl." The old woman now had a firm grip on Alice's arm and was looking up into her face, so Alice could see her broken teeth and black eyes. "She does what she has t' do t' survive, like we all does. We need her home."

"I know you do," Alice replied gently. "I don't know where she is or why they have her. I'm just a messenger. Go to the constable in Lydd if you need to."

"Paahh, you're right, you really don't know nothin' if you think them lot in Lydd would bother wi' Denge business."

"I'm sorry, you must be desperately worried. Perhaps if you told me why they have her then it would be easier for me to help."

The old hag tightened her grip, "All you need t' know is our Emily is a good woman and needs t' come home t' her rightful place beside her husband. The poor man is in a miserable way and how will we survive the winter if a strong man like him don't have the will t' go out fishin'?"

"I understand," said Alice, "Truly I do."

"Denge ain't like Dungeness, wi' strong men and decent boats. We've had bad luck wi' storms an' had our boats smashed up so they are only good for the fire. You know what bad luck breeds? More bad luck 'til most of us are gone to the grave or inland t' a new life. The rest of us cling on, doin' what we does to survive."

"What of the children?" Alice asked.

"What of the poor lil' blighters? Most of 'em don't live beyond a year and who can blame 'em? Who'd want t' live this life?"

Alice pondered on this and finally replied, "I don't know." She wondered how many children there were at Denge, not many she presumed. "Where do they go to school?"

"School?" the old woman cackled. "Do you think we can waste time on school? Sometimes they have to walk miles t' collect enough wood for the fire or go inland t' steal a nice chicken for dinner. Denge people don't have the need for fancy learning, waste of time, tha's what it is."

115

"Well, you never know what help it could be to read and write..." Alice began tentatively.

"So they turn out fancy an' leave me to fend for meself? No, you leave your teachin' for them the other side of the point." She took her gnarled hand off Alice's arm and stepped back. "You're no use to me, we'll find her though; we look after our own at Denge."

Alice took her chance to move on and soon the old hag was wisp in the mist and then no longer visible. She didn't call out and there was no more signs of Alice being followed. The familiar form of the lighthouse stood high, its top generating a weak light, guiding her in the direction of home. From the lighthouse the curve of the nearby station roof was her next beacon and from there the train tracks led her back.

The mist hung low over Dungeness for the next five days; a thick, damp, mass that rolled and twirled in the breeze. Fishermen were forced to leave their boats on the shingle beach and to stay bound to the land making repairs to their nets, boats or cottages. At first they often gathered at the Britannia or Pilot, lamenting the lack of fresh fish at their tables. Then by the Thursday, they sat beside their fires at home, no cash left in their pockets for the pub.

At the school, children came through the mist appearing like sprites and after school, disappearing quickly into an eerie darkness. It was mid-November and the days were becoming shorter. In the schoolhouse, neither Alice nor Hazel ventured out in the afternoons or evenings, instead they made small repairs to clothes, read books and wrote letters. Alice was very grateful for Hazel's company and although it irritated her to acknowledge it, also grateful to Tom Barton for making the arrangement.

Whether they were teaching or relaxing in the schoolhouse, whenever there was a quiet moment the rhythmic sound of the fog trumpet travelled across to them. It was the first thing Alice heard when she woke in the morning and the last thing she heard at night.

One evening, Alice wrote to Albert, knowing this was the first of her three letters that he would receive.

"We could go to Lydd on Saturday," Hazel suggested. "We'll go on the train together, post your letter and go to a teashop if you fancy."

"That would be wonderful," replied Alice.

It may not be Ashford; she knew Lydd was a very small town. However, it would have a church, shops and pavements, so that was good enough for Alice!

Dear Albert,

When this letter reaches you I will be quite settled at Dungeness, having been here two weeks. I do miss you, Mother and Father very much though and hope this letter finds you all well.

The school is a good, sound building, with one class of mixed ages, boys and girls. I am very much enjoying teaching and it is not so different from my own school-days. I live in the schoolhouse which is attached and I have a teachers' assistant, named Hazel, who shares the teaching accommodation with me. The headteacher is a Mrs Stubbs who lives in the nearby town of Lydd and travels here daily.

It's an unusual place, here at Dungeness, and not at all like Hythe or Broadstairs. It is a shingle headland and the whole area is pebbles. There are no trees or flower gardens. I long for our country views and pretty walks through the water meadows. The people are mainly fishermen and their families, or those living at the lighthouse.

Next weekend, Hazel and I are going by train to Lydd and I'll post this letter then. It's not a grand town like Ashford, but I shall enjoy the outing. In four weeks time I shall be home for the Christmas holiday break, which I am looking forward to very much. In the meantime, I look forward to receiving letters from you all.

With my fondest thoughts, your Alice.

Chapter Thirteen

Alice woke on Saturday morning feeling light-hearted at the prospect of an outing to Lydd. She had only been living at Dungeness for two weeks, but it felt like two months, and she still had the long winter ahead of her. But of course it was not just that she had been away from home for two weeks; it was as if she had been trapped in this comfort-less place. Was she being fanciful? Had she relished *Jane Eyre* so many times that she saw mystery where there was none? No, the horror of the body on the shingle and the letters home unsent were very real. Now Alice lived her very own mystery story and she longed to escape it.. A trip out was just what she needed and would raise her spirits for the coming week.

With an extra service running on a Saturday morning they could leave on the quarter-past ten train, then return on the quarter-past two from Lydd. Four whole hours away, Alice was bursting with anticipation! But first there was washing to be done and the young women heated water, pummelled their clothes and pulled them through the mangle in the outside shed. Finally, they pegged them on the line to dry in the brisk wind.

Alice insisted on wearing her smart boots when they set out for the railway station. Hazel laughed at her vanity, but then did the same! For Alice it was also a chance to wear her warm tweed skirt, a blouse with a lace collar and a cardigan rather than the severe black dress of a teacher. She added a pretty brooch and felt ready to explore the town.

"It's only Lydd," Hazel said, "Not somewhere fancy like Hythe or Canterbury."

"I don't mind," Alice said brushing her hair until it shone. "I'm just thrilled to be going out after being entombed in all this mist."

"Maybe we'll get a fringe cut for you," suggested Hazel. "Make your hair pretty, like that young woman we saw, you remember the one with the red hair?"

Alice did remember, of course. She had little else to think of whilst the mist hung heavy in the air. An unformed plan was brewing to make contact with Emily, but that was for another time. Today was a day for having fun, exploring a new place and allowing the tension to ease from her body.

The robust little tank engine backed in front of the station. It pulled one coach and only one person alighted. For the people of Dungeness this ten-fifteen departure was an ideal time to visit the shops, friends or family in Lydd, New Romney or further afield. There were several people waiting to step into the coach; Alice and Hazel found themselves sitting with an old woman who clutched a sturdy shopping basket.

The whistle blew and almost simultaneously the engine gave the first turns of its huge heavy wheels; the coach lurched forward and they were on their way, being pushed rather than pulled by the tank engine. By the time they passed the school, the engine was picking up speed. Alice was curious to see everything she had missed on the day she arrived. This time the sky was clear and windows free from condensation.

As the train moved onwards, Alice noticed the vegetation increased but for some time the ground was clearly still shingle. She first noticed fields in the distance to her left and then, as the engine moved onwards, fields reached the track-side. Finally, when the chimneys on the buildings and the pinnacles on the church tower were clear for her to see, the railway track itself was flanked by fields on both sides. They slowed as the orange brick station buildings came into view and most of the passengers alighted, pausing for a moment to reacquaint themselves with their surroundings.

For Alice this was her first view of Lydd; she could hardly include the distorted images seen through the misted window on the day of her arrival. It was a pleasant enough station, just as one would expect for a very small rural town. The station staff were smart and the area looked to be well cared for.

"I'll show you the town," Hazel said, as she led the way out and onto the main road. "It's no distance at all."

Keeping the tall church tower to their right, Hazel led Alice first to the green known as The Rype. It was an odd sort of place, rather vast for a village or town green with a sparse covering of grass and some stunted pine trees. Houses surrounded the area: some terraces and individual houses, including some attractive properties which looked to be quite old. They walked part way along and then crossed it by using one of many tracks. Children played in groups with balls and hoops, and Alice conceded that it made a wonderful playground for them.

When they sat down for lunch at *The George Hotel* two hours later, Alice was self-consciously displaying soft curls framing her face, and tickling her forehead.

"You can twist your hair in rags at night and you'll have lovely curls in the morning," Hazel advised her.

"I've just never had it like this before," Alice's fingers explored the curls "It will take a little getting used to but I can still put grips in to hold it back when I'm teaching."

"Or that pretty hair grip you just bought, that will do nicely."

Alice opened her handbag and took out the silver clip with a flower head of seed pearls and smiled, "It is pretty; I'll wear it tomorrow."

They decided to treat themselves to a roast dinner at the hotel. Hazel was thrilled to have mutton when so much of her diet consisted of fish. Plates and serving dishes were now empty.

"Are you going to have another cider?" Hazel asked, as she drained the last of her half pint glass.

"Oh no, I never... I mean I wouldn't usually have even the one. It's just tea for me."

"A pot of tea and fruit pie for two," Hazel said as the waitress approached.

"Very well, madam," the young woman replied.

"Listen to that," Hazel whispered as the waitress moved away. "She called me madam and she must be a year older than me!"

Alice smiled, it was good to be somewhere new and having fun. They had already seen the church, which really was quite large, the longest in Kent, Hazel had said. On a more serious note they had looked for and found the new grave of the unknown woman found on the beach. Then they had explored the shops, spending time looking through the ribbons and jewellery before Alice bought her hair-clip and Hazel treated herself to a brooch. For Alice though, the highlight of the day was finally to be able to post letters to her parents and Albert from the town post office.

"Lydd, Lydd. All alight for Lydd. Next stop Dungeness," the station master called out as the train eased to a stop alongside the platform. Doors were flung open and passengers stepped out, many of them in their best clothes, having been on a rare trip to Ashford. Porters stood to attention by their trolleys.

Alice and Hazel stepped into the coach. They were joined by another five or six women, all with shopping baskets bursting with the luxuries to be found in the town. One of them was Peggy Webb.

"I got a nice bit o' beef," Mrs Webb called across to someone sitting across the aisle.

"Did you now, my Bert he asked for bacon he did; I've got a joint to roast for tomorrow, we'll have it cold on Monday and the rest in a soup with split peas." This was one of the lighthouse keepers' wives; they lived in one of the houses circling the base of the tall building.

"I've got mutton, a big ol' bit as it's got to do the teachers as well," Peggy Webb nodded towards Alice and Hazel. "I'm cookin' for three of 'em now. I'll cook it at mine tomorro' then mince it for Monday, then a bit o' smoked bacon on Tuesday, after that it's fish for the week."

"That sounds lovely, Mrs Webb," Alice said. She had decided to revert to addressing the daily help in a formal manner.

"You've had your hair done different," Mrs Webb suddenly announced, causing everyone to turn in their seats to stare at the young teacher.

123

"Yes... well, yes just a little different." Alice looked down at her hands in her lap and twisted her 'diamond' ring.

A few minutes later and they were passing the school. How close Alice had passed to her new home and place of work, just two weeks before, and not even noticed it through the driving rain.

"Are you liking teaching here, in our school?" asked a middle-aged woman, the landlady of the Britannia pub.

"Yes, very much." Alice replied, as they approached Dungeness Station. "I like it very much indeed."

Quite a crowd of them all got off the train together, pausing to slip on their back-stays, baskets and bags at their feet. It was Peggy Webb with those sharp eyes of hers who first noticed the crowd beyond the lighthouse.

"There's a fair old crowd over there." She paused waiting for the others to look up. "I don't see no reason why anyone would be wanting to gather over on the point unless..."

"You're right, Peg. We'd best go an' see what's been going on while we've been out enjoyin' ourselves." The landlady from the Britannia stepped down from the station platform, "If there's been trouble then you can be sure I'll be busy behind the bar tonight."

"You're right there," Peggy was at her heels. "We'll want to get together and talk it through."

The two young women followed in the wake of the older women. They didn't speak to one another, but the feeling of apprehension in the pit of Alice's stomach foretold another tragedy. By the time they reached the point, it was clear to see there was a circular crowd around something… or someone. Peggy and the landlady had managed to push their way in amongst the crowd; Alice and Hazel could only stand at the perimeter, just getting a glimpse of a bundle of rags on the ground.

"Do you think it's another…?" whispered Hazel to Alice.

"I really don't know," Alice didn't want to assume. How could it be possible that there was now a third body in a matter of two weeks?

"Well, who is it then?" Peggy Webb asked.

"We don't know," Bess Stevens replied. "But it looks like she's been here for a while and she's not been swept up from the sea, not all the way up here on the bank.

"Unless she was alive and climbed up here, looking for help," someone else suggested.

"I've been walking straight past here these last few days," Mr Stevens said. "But the mist was that heavy I just walked the best I could from lighthouse to fog trumpet. She's in a dip you see, so even on a good day, if I wasn't looking in that direction…"

"Has someone gone for the vicar?" Alice asked, finding her voice from somewhere.

It was at that point the tight circle shifted as they turned towards Alice, giving her a clearer view of the body.

"Yes, I sent my Victoria and Bill," Bess came and gave Alice's arm a pat, sensing that it was a shock for the young woman.

"But, I think…" Alice took a step forward. "I think I know who she is."

Incredulous that the new teacher could possibly identify the body laid sprawled upon the shingle, they stepped back allowing her to come in amongst them.

"Yes, it's a woman from Denge." Alice looked down at the bundle of ragged skirt and tatty shawl. There was something about the way she lay... something about her leg... yes, that was it, she must have fallen and broken her leg or hip because her body was twisted at an odd angle. The gnarled, brown skinned hand still clutching at her shawl, the wizened old face and the tiny body with the hunched back – yes this was the old hag who had followed Alice from Denge when the sea mist blanketed the land.

Alice could feel her head spinning and the words forming could no longer be expressed. She was encircled by a blur and everything went into slow motion. Bess Stevens had been watching her closely, and was there to break her fall. And then others were holding her too and lowering her to the ground.

"Can someone cover the body?" Mr Stevens said, his voice breaking into Alice's consciousness. His tone commanded action.

The next thing Alice became aware of was Bess and Hazel on either side of her, supporting her as she sat on the shingle ridge.

"I'm sorry," Alice said.

"Don't say another word, dear." Bess was rubbing Alice's hands, presumably concerned she would become chilled after the shock.

So Alice sat, huddled up, looking at the body covered with the old woman's own shawl. Within a few minutes there was movement to her left and she turned to see the vicar, who was walking past the lighthouse and almost with them. He was escorted by Victoria and Bill Stevens, but also joining the party was Tom Barton and another man. They were carrying a ladder.

The vicar knelt beside the body of the old woman and said a short prayer. The heads of the onlookers were bowed and they fell silent. Then, with help from Tom Barton, he rose to his feet and said:

"Well, oh dear, this is unexpected, what a shame, what a sad day indeed it is."

"Miss Tibbs knows who she is," someone announced.

Again, all eyes were on Alice, who really felt she should be standing, but couldn't quite manage.

"I… yes… she is from Denge. I met her just a few days before."

"Well Miss Tibbs, then you must help me tell her family as you are acquainted." The vicar smiled with relief. "The men will carry her back home and we'll have to break the sad news."

"I don't even know her name," Alice said helplessly. "I just met her, that's all… I just met her out here on the Point. She is the aunt of the young woman who is missing. Emily Barton. Her husband was looking for her last week."

There were murmurs of acknowledgement. Did they know, Alice wondered, did they know it was because they held Emily the woman was dead? She had followed Alice back through the mist to try to learn where her niece was and it must have been after they parted that she had fallen. Perhaps Alice had still been a short distance away, but the mist muffled sounds and walking on the shingle was noisy. It may well have been that she had called out for help and not been heard.

"She was here looking for her niece and that is why she is dead." Alice's voice rang out loud and clear.

Now they were all silent and Alice knew every one of them (possibly excepting the vicar) knew that the woman was dead because they had taken her niece. They knew that they were to blame for the old woman's death. They also knew why they had Emily and this was still a mystery to Alice.

Tom Barton was the first to speak, "We'll get on with carrying her back to Denge then."

"And Miss Tibbs will come back to the cottage with me," Bess said. "She's just fainted and not fit to be walking out there and back again. A cup of tea by my fire and then these young women can walk back to the schoolhouse."

"Quite right, Mrs Stevens. Poor Miss Tibbs, we must look after you." The vicar nodded frantically.

As the onlookers turned their back on the dip within the shingle ridges, the frail body was placed upon the ladder. With ease it was lifted and so the small procession made its way towards Denge; just the two men with the ladder as a stretcher and the vicar in their wake.

Chapter Fourteen

The atmosphere back at the schoolhouse was subdued; all talk of how Alice had met the old woman of Denge had been thoroughly exhausted between the three women whilst drinking tea at Bess Stevens' home. Alice had told her friends that she had merely been walking on the point when the woman had appeared through the mist and begged her to help find her niece. They had parted and this was all Alice had to tell. What had happened next was pure speculation. Alice was unsure as to whether either Bess, Hazel or both knew of the whereabouts of Emily. It could be hard to read these Dungeness people; they clutched their secrets close to their hearts.

Now the young women were apparently absorbed with the work of bringing in their washing and started on the laborious business of ironing their clothes. The curtains were closed tight and they were cocooned in their own detached world for the evening. Bread toasted with cheese followed the ironing, and it was while they were washing up there was a knock on the door. Alice was half expecting it; they would never let it lie that she had seen the body of Emily on the shingle and were compelled to draw her into their plot.

"There's to be a meeting at the vicar's house and my brother says you are to come." Lucie Barton blurted out as soon as the door was opened. "The vicar says so too. You were the last to see her."

Lucie Barton didn't ask; there was an expectation on Alice to do whatever Tom Barton ordered. It was as if she were nothing but a pawn in a game where the fishermen, lighthouse keepers and their wives were the all-powerful playing pieces.

"I'll get my coat." Alice turned to Hazel, "The vicar is wanting to see me as I was the last person to see the woman. I'll go over now and be back within the hour I hope."

It was midnight-black, with a million tiny diamonds shining bright in the sky. The air was biting cold with a strong smell of sea-salt snapping at Alice's nostrils. The teacher felt a great deal of antipathy towards Tom Barton's sister, and this irritated her as there was no real reason. Lucie Barton was merely a messenger, just as Alice had been last week when she went to Denge. Alice wasn't inclined to speak and Lucie made no attempt either, so they slid across the stones in silence.

They passed the Britannia, and could hear voices raised as the topics of the day were discussed. Unlike the cottages, the windows were not curtained or shuttered and so a warm glow of light was emitted from each window, and Alice could see the people within. Stopping at the vicarage, they propped their back-stays against the ship-lap wall, where they joined another three pairs of the flat wooden boards.

Lucie raised the latch and opened the door. They stepped into a stifling heat, scented with the pungent smell of burning wood, enriched with overtones of ale and sweet sherry. Alice tried to welcome the heat but longed to leave the door thrown open and breathe fresh, cool air. Four pairs of eyes turned towards the newcomers but it was only the elderly vicar who raised himself from his armchair to

130

welcome the young women.

"Ah, Miss Barton and Miss Tibbs, come to discuss this poor woman from Denge," he said. "How kind, how very kind indeed. We have two chairs ready for you, and a sherry… you'll have a sweet sherry?"

They nodded politely and sat in the spare wooden upright chairs, so the six of them formed a circle with the book-laden side tables between them.

"Miss Tibbs, Connie and Ben Webb." Tom Barton made the introductions.

Alice smiled weakly and clutched at the stem of her sherry glass. "You're related to Mrs Webb, my daily help?"

"She's my aunt by marriage," Ben Webb replied.

"You said that the poor woman, God rest her soul, was looking for her niece. So sad she was worried about her when I have just learned that Mr and Mrs Webb here have been looking after poor Mrs Brooks who has been very sick." The vicar summed up what he knew, and to be fair it was a true version of events, but not the whole truth.

"It's time to return Emily Brooks to Denge but not before we've had a little chat with her husband and got him to see the error of his ways." Tom Barton addressed the gathering.

"May I ask what he has done?" Alice asked. "He lives in a one-room shack with an open fire and boarded up windows. What crime has he committed in order to. led to his wife being kept from him for two weeks?"

"Murder." Tom Barton's reply came with no embellishment.

"Murder?" Alice repeated, her throat tightening and mouth dry. She took a sip of the sherry, "He has a

131

temper, but murder? Who?"

"Not so much going out and killing with a knife or a musket," Ben Webb informed. "But it's murder nonetheless when you go out to try and stop the lifeboat men from doing their jobs and that causes lives to be lost, which could have been saved."

"It's murder if you push a captain or one of the crew overboard if they try to stop you getting at their cargo." Tom Barton commented looked straight at Alice as if challenging her to disagree.

Alice felt horror ripping through her body and shivered despite the stifling heat in the vicarage. "What is he then, this Ed Brooks? A wrecker or a smuggler?"

"Now, don't you go getting smuggling confused with wrecking. For all your education you maybe don't understand that smuggling isn't theft and there's no need for anyone to get hurt. No, a smuggler is an honest man who takes nothing but a bit o' tax from those that have more than enough money in their silk-lined purses. No, we are not talkin' about smuggling and not wrecking either..." Ben Webb paused for effect, "We're talkin' about landing on boats in trouble, boats who have sent a signal for help, and going along and helping themselves to a little of what the captain and his crew can't take care of whilst they are fighting for their lives."

"Piracy?" Alice whispered.

"Not them pirates from yer story books, but similar, yes. Just sitting around, watching and waiting, then out they go on their little boats and land alongside."

"Ed Brooks does this on his own?" Alice asked.

"Him and his no-good cousin, Jake Brooks." Tom replied, "They are all at it though, watching and

132

waiting and now it looks like they take the women too, if they are fit enough. Why else was that wife of his washed up on the beach?"

"I've been to Denge," Alice said, "and it's a desperate place. They live in one room hovels; the children don't go to school but spend their days scavenging for firewood and food."

"There's no excuse for murder," Tom snapped.

"No, I just… I just mean to say that they have been pushed to take desperate measures to feed their families."

"They know the tides and the currents, especially round the point. Where one ship may be floundering, it's nothing to them to put out a little boat and pull up alongside it. There's no one tougher hereabouts than those Brooks cousins." Ben told it so Alice could see it all: the floundering ships and the ruthless pirates circling, waiting to go in for their loot.

"What do they get from a ship in trouble, two men and a small boat?" Alice was curious, thinking of their hovels and realising that whatever they did, it was not leading to any great comfort in their lives.

"A sack of grain, a thick coat or a blanket is enough for them to push a sailor overboard. They are not expecting money or jewels, those rats will settle for anything." Ben Webb paused for a slug of ale, "A life for a cask of ale or a bale of wool, it's not right."

"They make it harder for the lifeboat crews," the bitterness in Tom's voice was clear. "The boat in danger might think they are coming to save them or we've had them blocking our path, trying to get away as we arrive. Ed and Jake only go for a boat that they can get to, before us or the Rye crew."

"She's not a bad lass, that Emily," Connie Webb added, "she just got caught up with a nasty lot."

"Emily was out there, the night when I arrived and the lifeboat had been called," Alice reflected. "What was she doing? Helping them? She went overboard and nearly drowned, ended up here at Dungeness… half dead she was and you cared for her, but why? Why not take her back for them to look after? Why care if she lived or died?"

"She were left on the boat that night," Connie said. "They need all the help they can get and, with her on board, that leaves Ed and Jake to take over the troubled ship. They can't go leaving their own boat all alone, stands to reason they need more help."

"There's one good thing about Ed Brooks – he loves that woman with a passion," Tom Barton said. "She may be the one to set him straight."

"Or if she's kept from him for long enough, he may well agree to anything to get her back," Alice concluded.

All this time the vicar had sat half dozing in his chair. Alice wondered what went on in his confused mind. Was he as involved as everyone else in the plan to hold Emily against her will or had they included him at the last minute, so as to add a degree of respectability to the meeting? As a man of the cloth, did he condone kidnapping? For that was what it was, whatever the reason.

The small group had fallen silent for a moment, reflecting on the words said and opinions raised. It was then that the vicar spoke with unusual clarity:

"Young Mr Barton, it seems as if you are the one to go to that pitiful place and see this Mr Brooks. I fear that our Mr Webb is a little too angry to resolve this. Of course, Miss Tibbs must go too. Her presence will keep Mr Brooks calm, I am sure."

"I really don't see…" Alice began.

"Of course you don't my dear." The old man looked over the top of his glasses at her. "But you are doing splendidly and are fast becoming one of us."

"Very well, I'll go to Denge with Mr Barton." Alice was becoming resigned to life becoming unpredictable.

Tom rose to his feet. "We'll be off to see this Ed Brooks then and if he sees sense and stops robbing innocent people then I'll bring him back to see his wife." He was fastening his overcoat and then pulling a hat on snug over his ears.

"We'll be seeing you shortly," Ben Webb said. "But it will be Connie who decides if she's fit to travel back to Denge."

"Fair enough," Tom replied.

With those parting words, Tom and Alice stepped out into the sharp evening air, pushed boots into back-stays and started the short journey to the west of the point. They didn't speak for a while other than for Tom to point out an obstacle in the path or to check Alice was comfortable with the pace. As the air was clear, there was no need to follow the coast so they passed the inland side of the lighthouse and then on to Denge.

"You got your letter posted?" Tom asked as the hovels of Denge became clear.

"At the post office in Lydd," Alice confirmed. She didn't feel inclined to speak any further about the matter; she believed it was due to him or others like him that the first letters had not been sent.

Then they were nearly there. Alice could see the first building she had knocked at on her previous visit, that of the dead woman. Today it showed no light or smoke from a fire. Behind it was the hovel, home to Ed and Emily Brooks; at first it too seemed deserted but then Alice's attention was drawn to a grey trail of smoke coming from the chimney.

"It's this one," Alice said.

Tom rapped hard on the door. A scrape of a chair being pushed back and a shuffling noise could be heard and then Ed Brooks was at the door. Through the half-open doorway the inner stench of the fishing net, wood-smoke and unwashed body wafted out; a sharp contrast to the frosty fresh air. It was Ed who spoke first:

"Oh, it's you, Tom Barton, and that teacher who should know better than to get mixed up in Denge business. Haven't we had enough grief for one day, with Aunt Ida lying stiff in her home?"

"We have. Miss Tibbs and I are here to put an end to it. There's been enough death hereabouts recently and we've come to see if you are ready to talk sense."

"And Emily?"

"She can come back so long as."

"So you're here to barter are you?" Ed snarled. "You'd best come in an' say your piece."

They stepped into the hovel. There was no welcome from the warmth of the weak fire and again it was the only light in the room. The nets were dry, Alice noticed, but then of course with all this mist the fishing boats had been grounded for days. The Dungeness fleet would have been out as soon as the mist lifted, she was sure of that. Whereas Mr Brooks would not bother to stir himself.

"I've been talking to my cousin, Jake, and we'll not stand for Emily bein' kept any longer." Ed Brooks remained standing and didn't invite his guests to sit at the table which had a coating of crumbs and spilled ale or tea.

"You wife is much stronger now, maybe fit enough to travel home," Tom informed him.

"I'll come an' get her then." He took a step towards the door.

"Ready to come home when you've agreed to stop your pirating, you and your cousin."

Ed shook his mop of greasy black hair and eyes showed disgust. "Pirating? You and your tales, Tom Barton, where's me pile of gold an' casks o' brandy?"

"It doesn't have to be gold," Alice spoke quietly but both men turned to take notice. "If you go out and steal from ships who are in danger, if you pull up alongside them and take what you can while they fight for their lives, then it's stealing and stealing in a most horrible and heartless way."

"I have to feed my family an' the old folk here," Ed Brooks replied with a little less fight than before.

"So you'll push a sailor overboard or sail past someone floundering in the sea, just for a few coins, an overcoat or pair of boots. Maybe just for the food from their table?" Tom replied. He stood just as tall as Ed Brooks but his manner was a little milder. "Around the point we have two boats for going out and saving lives, and there's another at Rye Harbour. Here at Denge you and your cousin have a boat for robbing."

"I do it for the family. It's not much but it makes a diff'rence. I've got a boat that I share with Jake and the two of us can't provide for everyone here. The others are getting too old and their boats are rotting as we speak." Ed kicked at the floor. "This isn't bringing my Emily home. You've said your piece, now let me bring me wife home."

"You'll stop this robbing and your cousin Jake too," Tom said. "Then Emily can come home, although

I suggest you tidy the place up first."

"I thought there'd be a deal to be done and I'll do anything for my Emily, but it will mean telling her that we'll have to leave the coast and head inland for work."

"Very well, Mr Brooks," Alice said. "You may come and collect your wife, but I suggest you have a good wash and change into some cleaner clothes. Shall we expect to see you in the morning?"

"I'll be there within the hour," was the snarl of a reply.

"We'll be at Ben Webb's house," Tom said, as they left.

Chapter Fifteen

Emily Brooks was just as Alice had imagined her. She had seen her of course, but only as the fleeting beam of light had shone on her bedraggled body. She had been lying there as if she were dead and Alice had barely registered her existence before someone, presumably Ben Webb, had scooped her up from her bed of stones and tangled rope. A week later she had seen the glow of her auburn hair in the distance and was sure it was the same woman.

Now, here she was, Emily Brooks, sitting in the corner of the living room in the Webb's cottage. Her beautiful hair was tied back in a thick rope of a plait and coiled at the base of her slender neck. Grey eyes were in shadowed sockets and her face was pale; she looked haunted and weary. Her hands cradled a cup of tea and she sat with a thick shawl around her, despite the warmth from the range.

Alice nodded and forced a smile when they were introduced. Guilt settled uneasily in her stomach. Did Emily recognise her as the person who could have rescued her, but instead hid and allowed her to be taken? She wanted to explain, to say that she was new here herself, and scared... yes she had been too scared to help. How many times had she wished that she had stayed to see if the young woman was dead or alive?

"There now, your husband will be here within

the hour, he says," Connie bent low to hear the whispered reply for it seemed she was the only person Emily trusted enough to speak with. "He wanted to tidy himself up first, you know what men are like, they let things slip if we are not about to care for them."

"He has missed you terribly," Alice volunteered.

The large grey eyes just looked at Alice and then down at the tea. The two men, Ben and Tom, sat together at the plain dark wooden table; they spoke quietly and supped at tankards of ale. The women sat in the easy chairs.

Connie spoke to Alice about her teaching, the weather and the visit to Lydd earlier that day. It hardly seemed possible that only six hours before, Alice and Hazel had been eating roast mutton at The George Inn and life had seemed a little more carefree. They tried to include Emily in their conversation, asking if she had been to Lydd recently or what her own memories were of the little school amongst the shingle. Emily just nodded or whispered the occasional comment which could only be heard by Connie. She held her shawl tight as if to cocoon herself.

All the time they sat and talked, the foremost thought in everyone's mind was that Ed Brooks would soon be with them. Finally, within the hour, there was a knock on the door and Ben Webb answered it.

"You'd better come in."

He only had eyes for his Emily, that big angry man whose eyebrows were permanently knotted in a frown. In a couple of steps he was kneeling at her feet, his hands in hers, looking up into her face. Then he wrapped his big bear arms around her slender body and she began to cry. Finally, Ed sat on a stool beside his wife, still holding her hand, while she dried her tears on her shawl.

"She's been weak, with a temperature and a chill all at once." Connie began to speak gently, "She were that battered and bruised, but it's fading now. It's her spirits I worry about though, she's lost the baby and is that shaken up..."

"The baby? I didn't know." Ed looked into his wife's face but her eye-lids were lowered.

"I couldn't tell... I couldn't, how were we to manage?" Her voice was soft and she forced her gaze to meet his. They sat in silence for a moment.

"I'd never have let you take the boat, had I known," Ed began. "I'm sorry, I hadn't realised. I didn't know."

"She's been sitting out the back on good days," Connie said. "Well wrapped up but a bit of sunshine does the power of good."

"There's to be no more robbing," Ed told his wife. "I don't know how we'll manage, maybe I'll look for work in Lydd, but we'll put all that other stuff behind us, Jake too."

"I can't stop thinking about it, Ed, that boat over Rye way last summer, it had grounded itself on a sandbank, and then you boarded it – you an' Jake – and the captain, he put up a fight, an' then he was overboard and swimming towards me. I had to turn about, I could have saved him, but then it might have been me overboard. I watched him die, Ed."

"I know love. I know, but I did it for us and the others at Denge."

"What did you get for a man's life?" Ben Webb called across the room.

"Come on, Ben, we've got to move on from this," Tom said. "Let Emily say her piece and we'll leave it at that."

Emily's eyes filled with tears again. Her

141

husband looked at a loss as to how to comfort her. He sat on the stool at her side, looking at his good black boots – the captain's boots – and didn't have the words to tell her how he'd provide for her and keep her safe.

"Tom's right, love." Connie spoke gently, "We need to get you well and back home with your husband."

"I love him, but he's not my husband," Emily blurted out. "How could we afford to get wed? It's a blessing that this baby isn't to be born illegitimate, God rest its soul. He's a good man." She looked now at Ben Webb, "He's a good man really, Mr Webb, but I don't want to go back there, not back to Denge."

Silence fell upon the room; Ed Brooks sat with his head in his hands and Emily had pulled the protective shawl tighter around her body. Alice could only think of the double box-bed that ran along one side of the Brooks' hovel and she could not imagine what sinful intimacies might have taken place there. The two men at the table looked uncomfortable after the outburst; this was women's business and it was getting complicated. Everyone waited for Connie to deal with the latest revelation.

"It's getting late and Emily needs her rest." She stood up and bent down to take Emily's arm. "Come on now, this isn't helping you get better. We can talk about this tomorrow or whenever you feel ready."

Emily stood up and looking at Ed she said, "Thank you for coming, I'm sorry I can't come home yet."

The big man with the shock of dark hair just looked at his love and, as she left the room, he stood too, walked across the room, opened the door and was gone into the night.

Alice didn't pause to ask the others what should be done. She felt the man's grief as she had no doubt of his love for Emily. He had shown he had a temper but when it came to the woman he called his wife, there was nothing but tenderness. Alice was out of the door and before he had taken many long strides, she was calling after him.

"Mr Brooks, Ed, wait a moment… please."

He turned and waited for her to catch up.

"It's getting late and Emily is tired. Remember how ill she has been, she looks tired and weak. I've not met her before but I imagine she was strong and plucky."

"She was, but I'd nurse her back to health if only she'd let me."

"She loves you," Alice persisted. "Give her time and show her that a life in Denge is worth coming back to. You can visit her now you know where she is. But in the meantime, go out early tomorrow and catch some fish for the others that need you at Denge. In the late afternoon, I'll call on you and together we can make plans to bring Emily home."

"You're right," Ed replied, "I've not thought of anyone, my head has been so filled with my own worries. I'll make a home fit for Emily and she'll come back soon enough."

"You could do with a friend to help you. I'll be with you Sunday afternoon."

"I never thought I'd be needing a school teacher for a friend!" A smile broke through, he turned and was gone.

Alice turned back to the Webb's cottage. Suddenly she felt very weary and longed to be back at the schoolhouse. She hoped Hazel had put a warmed brick in her bed. Opening the door of the cottage, she closed it behind her, but stood at the doorway. It was just Tom and Ben there, still sitting at the table.

"I just said to him that he needs to get out on his boat before low tide in the morning. He needs to make an effort so she'll want to come home. I'll go over to see him later and see what can be done to make the place more respectable for Emily."

"That was good of you," Tom replied.

"I'm going now," Alice told them. "I'm tired."

She couldn't cut across the shingle, like the school children did; she wasn't familiar enough with the terrain to go across it at night. It was back to the lighthouse and then the station before finding the railway tracks leading home to the school.

"Friends and neighbours. As we gather here today and give thanks for our own health and the good harvest of fish that has blessed our fishermen in the last few days, we must also pray for one that is less fortunate." The vicar leant upon the side of the pulpit, and closed his eyes before beginning the prayer.

"Dear Lord, we pray for our neighbour, Ida Thomson, that she may have a smooth journey to the afterlife and bask in the light of your care. May her family and friends turn to you in their grief and find comfort from their faith. Amen."

The small congregation muttered their response. Then without further announcement the vicar launched into 'Abide With Me' and the old fisherman on the piano struggled to keep pace.

Sunday morning had come too quickly for Alice, after a restless night pondering over the fate of Ed and Emily Brooks. She was relieved when the church service was over and quickly moved through the connecting door rather than make conversation

144

with the curious locals. It would all be about the body of Ida Thomson and how Alice had been the last to see her. She wasn't going to go through it all again, no, a cup of tea and a couple of chapters of *Northanger Abbey* would suit her far better. Hazel had gone to spend the rest of the day with her family and so Alice settled down to read.

After her midday meal, Alice gathered a basket and filled it with soap, a scrubbing brush and various cloths. She wrapped half a fruit cake, added a few of the apples from Mrs Stubbs' garden and a jar of jam. A large apron was taken from a hook on the wall and placed on the top of the basket. She set off across the shingle at a fair pace on her back-stays.

On reaching the point, Alice could see some activity at Denge. It seemed that the people who lived there had come out of their winter hibernation. Although the only fair-sized fishing boat was now up on the beach, it was clear it had been out on the very early morning tide. A small group of three children and a couple of elderly women were sorting through the catch, tossing some aside and keeping others. The men, Ed and presumably Jake, were pulling out the huge net and placing it over the shingle. A young woman and a toddler picked off bits of seaweed.

Ed looked up and on seeing Alice he moved away from the others. "Good day, Miss Tibbs. We've got some cod an' a bit o' pollock. Enough to feed us lot for a few days an' some to be smoked. If we do as well tomorrow there'll be enough spare to take into Lydd."

"Wonderful. Was it dreadfully cold out there?"

"It usually is!" Ed grinned at her. "Our Helen, that's Jake's wife over there, she said we should put the net in with Ida, it's not like she'll be minding."

"In with Ida?" Alice was confused.

145

"We'll set up some hooks an' use her place as a net store. We don't need it for anything else."

Alice could see this was an excellent plan, to remove the nets from hanging in his home would make a big difference, reducing the fishy smell and giving much-needed space. There was something different about Ed too, his beard had been trimmed, not professionally but it was shorter and smarter.

Ed saw her looking and said, "Helen did it, gave me hair a tidy up." He removed his woollen hat and showed a shorter, if not neater, head of black curls.

"We'd best get on then," Alice indicated to her basket. Then she looked towards the industry on the beach. "Shall I make a start if you are needed here?"

"No," he replied firmly. "When you go back I want you to tell Emily that I helped tidy up and that I'm doing my best to make this place the home she deserves."

Two hours later, the iron hooks had been removed from the ceiling beam and all traces of seaweed and debris fallen from the nets had been scrubbed from the floor, ceiling and boards across the window. The whole floor had been washed and the rag rug had been taken outside and vigorously beaten.

There was a fair collection of driftwood logs in a small shed and Alice found a basket, in need of repair but useful to put beside the hearth for the logs. The food cupboards were almost bare but all food was taken out, checked for crawling insects and returned to a clean shelf.

When Alice left she took with her two blankets, which she was determined to wash and dry, despite the short days and frequent lingering mist. She would wash two a week she had told him and suggested he made the same effort with his own clothes. Ed Brooks meekly agreed to all her demands.

Dear Mother,

I hope this letter finds you and Father in good health. I have become involved in an effort to improve one of the cottages of a local family. They are very poor, coming from a fishing family, and relying on two men and one boat to feed and support both their extended families. The wife of one, her name is Emily, has been ill and is being cared for by another local family. In order to bring her back to her own family I am helping to make improvements to her own home, so as to raise her spirits.

I was thinking of the blue curtains we had hanging in our dining room. They were very faded from the sun but could be taken apart and re-stitched to fit much smaller windows. Would you be so kind as to ask Martha to pack them up for me? If you had any spare sheets, they would also be very welcome.

I will sign off now and look forward to seeing you within a couple of weeks when I return for Christmas.

Much love, Alice.

Chapter Sixteen

"I saw you, on the shingle that night. I thought... I thought you were dead. Did you see me? Did you know it was me?" Alice had rehearsed the words over and over but when she finally saw Emily on her own, the words came no easier for all her practice. "I didn't know... I was going to help."

"I don't recollect," Emily's frown was deep. "Maybe you can tell me, help me to remember."

Another week had passed, probably the most uneventful since Alice's arrival. There was nothing to be done to help Ed Brooks in the evenings, as darkness was already falling by the time the pupils left school; it was not sensible to walk around the point and little to be achieved from it. The blankets had been washed on the morning after Alice had brought them back to the schoolhouse and had dried in the strong winds that brought no rain. Alice had plucked them off the gorse bushes where they had landed having escaped the restraints of the clothes pegs and placing them on the airer above the range had ensured they were totally dry.

Now, on Saturday morning, Alice had the clean blankets in her basket and decided to visit Emily before going to Denge. On nearing Ben and Connie Webb's cottage she had recognised Emily seated outside, huddled up with the cottage as her windbreak. Alice sat down beside her and received a weak smile.

"I'm sorry, I had to tell you how sorry I am, even though you don't remember. There is no excuse for walking away."

"Perhaps you were frightened?" Emily looked calmer today, a little less tired and anxious.

"I was," Alice admitted. "I'd just arrived, I didn't know what to expect. It was so different. I came from Ashford."

"You're the new teacher; Connie told me about you. You were there on the beach that night, can you tell me about it?"

"I had been to see the vicar and he said I needed to go to the schoolhouse." Alice began. "I didn't know the way, and it was dark. The rain had stopped but the sky was overcast, then there was the light from the lighthouse, blinding me every few seconds. I was struggling with the shingle, we have paths in Ashford. I tripped and there you were."

"I was lying there on the shingle, by the vicar's home?"

"Do you know how you got there?"

"I got swept into the sea and the boat came back, smashin' against me, sending me down... I kicked my way up and I knew I couldn't get back to Denge," Emily's head was in her hands as if heavy with the burden of remembering. "I know these currents though and I let it carry me to Dungeness beach. I remember pullin' meself up the bank, out of the way of the tide-line."

"But your husband... Ed, he said that you went missing on a Friday night and I saw you late Saturday afternoon," Alice paused to reflect. "No wonder you were close to death, you'd been there half the night and all the following day."

"Connie didn't think I'd make it." Emily pulled

her shawl closer. "I must have woken and pulled meself up towards the cottages, I don't remember." She began to stand, "I'm getting cold, time to go in… would you…?"

"No. I'll be on my way. I'm going to see Ed; he's tidying your home. Making it nicer for you."

"That's kind of you to help," Emily said, "but you don't need to make amends, I know what it's like to be afraid and lost."

It took about twenty minutes to reach Denge from the Webbs' cottage. Alice's heart was pounding from the exertion; she would be grateful to sit for a moment with Ed Brooks. For all that he had a temper and was the tallest, broadest man she knew, Alice felt no fear of him. She hadn't really thought he would harm her the night they first met, when he was searching for his wife. Alice believed his love for Emily softened him and, when he was with her, it made him think before he allowed his temper to take hold. She was looking forward to seeing him, hoping that he was still positive about the future.

There was no smoke coming from the chimney of Ed's shack and no activity on the beach. The boat belonging to the Brooks' cousins was pulled high on the beach beyond high tide mark. Alice rapped on the door of the shack, but she already sensed that no one was home. Lifting the latch she tentatively opened the door and peeped in.

It was with relief that Alice saw that the place was in good order, with the table and sink area clear of food debris and unwashed implements. The smell from the open fire could not be avoided, but the stench of seaweed and rotting fish had gone. She placed the freshly laundered and folded blankets on the table and

150

took a reel of tape from the basket. Reaching up to take the measurements of the two windows, Alice jotted the figures down in her notepad.

Next Alice stripped the two blankets from the bed, holding them away from her and dropped them, unfolded, into her basket. Then she reached over the bed to straighten the sheets before replacing the blankets. She longed to plunge the sheets into a copper of soapy water, but that was for when her mother had sent replacements.

Alice was so occupied with her endeavours that she didn't hear the creak of the door as it opened or the scrape as it scuffed against the uneven floor. She was leaning across the bed, in a way that she would not have done had Ed Brooks been present, for slender ankles and stockinged calves were on display. When the door slammed shut she turned quickly, expecting Ed, but found herself sitting on the box bed looking up into the scornful black eyes of Jake Brooks. He stood over her, so close that his legs almost touched her own, now hanging over the side of the box bed.

"What have we here? The school teacher in my cousin's bed whilst his wife is sick." He leered at her showing broken teeth and made no move to back away. "Miss Tibbs, not so prim and proper now. I wondered what you were up to comin' around here with yer fruit cake and yer scrubbin' brush. Makin' the place cosy were you? And for what? So you could get Edward into bed with you?"

She said nothing, but stared back at him, cornered like a wild animal in a trap. She was sickened by his insinuations although barely understanding the meaning of them.

"You think he'll come an' save you? He's gone

off to Lydd... be away for hours." Then seeing the fear mount in her eyes Jake continued, "No need to fret, if you're wanting a Brooks then one cousin is as good as another." Slowly he looked her up and down from newly cut fringe and neat mouth to her flushed neck, down the pin-tucked blouse to the glimpse of her stockings still on display. The predator eased forwards, his knee between hers, stopping Alice from covering herself and causing her to lean back away from him.

"No need to be so eager," he laughed briefly as she blushed furiously, mouth so dry she was unable to speak and knowing that to scream was pointless. "I've not decided if you're to my taste... I like my women with a bit more flesh on them, but they say a change is good."

Alice turned her face away, so she couldn't see his leering over her or smell his rank breath. As he leaned closer, placing a hand on her waist, Alice found her voice:

"I'm not here for your cousin, he is as good as married so keep your foul thoughts to yourself. I'm engaged to be married in the summer."

"Engaged to be married are you? Well, your man would thank me for teaching you a thing or two." He took her chin and turned her face so their eyes met. "He'll thank me very much indeed."

Jake moved back slightly, leaving Alice lying defenceless on the bed. As he stood straight he began to shrug off his braces and his breeches fell to his feet. In sick horror she felt compelled to watch and so saw the cottage door open behind him and her first thoughts were not that she was to be saved but that her reputation would be tarnished forever.

Just as previously Alice had been unaware of

152

Jake entering the hovel, he had not heard the two men enter. She saw his eyes wide with horror as a hand – Ben Webb's she thought – clamped down on his shoulder. There was a brief howl of protest as Jake was pulled back, a crack as his head hit the table top and a thud as his body hit the floor.

Alice drew her legs up to her stomach and crouched on the bed, her face on her knees, unable to look at her rescuers. The shame at what they had seen burned within her.

"Get up and home to your poor wife," Ben Webb snarled at the fallen man. "Get up and explain why you've got yourself one hell of a headache."

"I don't think he can." It was Tom Barton who spoke next. Still Alice sat, hunched up with her eyes tightly closed as if to open them would make the scene become real.

"He's not... he's tougher than that... he's...." That was Ben, Alice could hear, she didn't want to hear him though, she wanted to be shut away from them all.

"Look at his eyes; they're the eyes of a dead man." There was a silence whilst Tom moved to the body on the floor. "He's not breathing."

"You think he's..."

"I don't doubt it," Tom muttered. "He always was a bloody piece of filth, but this was an accident. By God, we won't hang for ridding the world of Jake Brooks. I'll not have it. We've got to move him before the blood stains through the rug. There's no time to stand around discussing it. We'll roll him up in it."

"And what about her?" Alice knew they were looking at her.

"She's all right. She won't see us rot for this." Tom spoke with confidence.

153

Alice still hadn't looked and they hadn't spoken to her. She heard the sound of the table moving and a rhythmic thud as the body was rolled up.

"I've got a better rug at home," Tom said, "We'll bring it along as a gift for Ed." Then Alice felt the bed give as he sat on the edge beside her and asked gently, "Did he hurt you?"

She shook her head but her voice was not strong enough to be heard.

"He's gone and there's no time to waste; we've got to get him out of here. There's no one about but that could change and we'll not be caught for this."

"But we can't... we've got to tell someone... the constable," Alice began.

"It was an accident; we never meant it to happen," Tom spoke slowly but clearly. "Do you want to tell the law, tell them what happened?"

Alice was stronger than she looked, after a lifetime of protection from her parents and conforming to people's expectations, she had known nothing but love and support before coming to Dungeness. She had helped her mother with the poorer families in their community and gained an inner confidence and strength not always obvious under her prim exterior. Since coming to Dungeness she had experienced a more savage way of life and rather than crush her, it had strengthened her further. Alice knew if she stayed curled up in a ball of despair, she put the lives of these good men at risk.

Alice stood up and turned to straighten the bed, then picking up her basket she looked at the men and said, "I've got these blankets to take back to wash."

She avoided looking at the bundle on the floor and opened the door, looking out around the cluster of houses. Then with a nod to the men to say it was clear, Alice stepped out onto the shingle.

Tom Barton and Ben Webb were both fishermen and lifeboat men, strong and broad, still young enough to cope with the rigours of their lives. But, Jake Brooks (fisherman and pirate) was a tall man and it took all their strength to hoist him over their shoulders and carry him away from Denge. Alice hadn't heard them discuss it, it seemed to be by unspoken agreement that they set off inland, avoiding the coast or going too close to the settlement at Dungeness. Every so often they paused for a moment but their load stayed on their shoulders and with a nod to one another they moved on.

After ten minutes, they came to a dip in the shingle and wordlessly the body was laid down. The three of them knelt and pushed away the stones to make a hollow pit deep enough to hold a man and a foot of shingle above him.

"Take the rug away, then if he's found there will be no evidence," as Alice spoke the words she knew they made her as guilty as the others for the crime. Aiding and abetting it was called.

"I'll burn it back at mine," Tom said. "And bring over the new one within the hour."

Three pairs of hands pulled at the piles of stones allowing them to pour over the body. It was soon covered and it was a relief to see no more trace of black hair, tatty material or the toe of a boot. Alice knelt at the graveside and prayed for the dead man's soul, whilst the men stood in silence, their heads bowed. Then they moved away, without looking back. They didn't speak at all until they reached the railway tracks, the point where the men would go back towards the coast and Alice to the school.

155

"This stays between the three of us; we never tell, not our wives nor sweethearts." Ben looked straight at Alice.

"Of course," she answered, a hint of defiance returning. How could he say that, how could she ever admit to what happened?

With no further words, the three of them separated. Alice moved on… one foot after the other… sliding over the shingle. Looking ahead but only seeing the slight hump in the shingle pit behind her.

For the following week the rain flung itself down upon the shingle headland, finding its way through gaps in window frames and under doors. Half-drowned children scurried into the school, their coats were then spread over drying racks by the fire, causing the atmosphere in the schoolroom to be humid. Skies were darkening by early afternoon and it was as black as midnight by the time the end of the school day.

Alice, burdened by headaches, struggled through the days and dreaded the nights where she was plagued by visions of Jake Brooks forcing himself upon her. She frequently woke with a jump, as the loud crack of his head hitting the table ricocheted around in her mind. She felt Peggy Webb's beady eyes upon her, wondering what was wrong. But for once Alice knew that Mrs Webb had no idea what went on in her troubled mind.

In the evenings, Alice and Hazel cut the thick dark blue velvet, which had arrived from the Ashford Rectory, and reshaped it into two smaller sets of curtains. It was hard work under the weak, fluttering light of the oil lamps. Alice was grateful for Hazel's company and support; she used her headache as an excuse for being quieter than usual.

Then on the Saturday morning, four weeks after her arrival, Alice woke and decided that she would no longer live her life in the shadow of guilt and shame. She had not encouraged him to assault her and she had no doubt that decent men should not hang for manslaughter. She was twenty years old and was going to do her very best to be a good teacher and, following that, a good wife. If the tiniest memory of what happened began to taunt her, then she would immediately think of apple trees in blossom and spring flowers. Yes, that is exactly what she would do.

She was the first to be out of bed and busied herself in opening the damper, putting logs on the stove and then the kettle on top. Hazel came through to the smell of frying bacon and tomatoes.

"You're feeling better then?" Hazel asked.

"Thankfully my headache has passed and I need to take these curtains to Denge. Will you come with me? The rain has stopped; it will be cold though as we have a frost. Can you believe it after all the rain? But see how pretty it is on the stones."

Chapter Seventeen

Dearest Albert,

At last I am coming home for Christmas! My train leaves at quarter-past ten on Saturday 22nd, and should be in Ashford by half-past eleven. If you can meet me at the railway station then I will be pleased to see you. If you are unable, then I am sure Mother and Father can collect me. I shall return on Saturday 5th January.

I am so looking forward to spending time with you all.

With love from your Alice.

Alice was hoping that her parents would be waiting for her on the station platform as the great, iron wheels came to a stop, and the buffers bumped against each other giving each coach a light jolt. She was standing steady, poised at the doorway and trying to peer out of the grubby window for a familiar face. One hand was on the brass handle and the other on her suitcase. She had opened the door before the porter reached it and stepped out onto the platform.

The air felt dirty from the numerous filthy great beasts that belched smoke into the station throughout the morning. The fine, ornamental station buildings and decorative ironwork all had a coating of soot in varying degrees. The platform was buzzing with the voices of passengers getting off the trains, passengers getting on the trains, people meeting friends and family or wishing them a safe journey. Station staff were carrying bags, pushing trolleys, answering queries and checking tickets. Alice felt momentarily stunned by the busy surroundings, although she was pleased, of course she was pleased, to be home for Christmas.

"Alice dear, Alice, over here."

Alice turned and there were her mother and father. Then she was in her mother's arms and her father was patting her arm awkwardly with one hand, whilst taking her suitcase with the other.

"I'm home," said Alice.

Within five minutes they were all in the trap, pulled by a pony Reverend Tibbs sometimes borrowed, and heading past the town centre, towards the green and leafy village of Willesborough. On turning into Church Road, Alice's attention was all set towards her first glimpse of the distinctive spire of her father's church, St Mary The Virgin. There it was: the tiled spire and what an impressive building it was with its triple roofs covering the nave and aisles. Then into the driveway of the substantial early Victorian vicarage.

"Albert couldn't leave work earlier, I assume," Alice had said to her mother. "I knew half-past eleven was a little early but I wondered..."

"He's working hard and saving for your future," her mother reproached her. "He'll be going home for a tidy up and with us for afternoon tea."

Now it was half-past two and Alice was sure Albert would be here soon. What would it be like, seeing him after seven long weeks? She looked down at her engagement ring. It would be wonderful, of course it would. Alice had put away her clothes, ironed the creases from her skirts and blouses. She had spoken with her parents and eaten a midday meal. Still Albert did not come and it was not until Martha was putting the teapot on the table that the doorbell rang and Martha was scuttling from the dining room to the hallway and the front door.

There he was – Albert. He removed his hat to reveal a neat centre parting and slicked brown hair; he looked to be freshly shaved, side burns neatly shaped. An overcoat was slung onto the coat rack; he wore a mid-brown two piece: trousers and a waistcoat. His white shirt was freshly laundered and a tie gave the appearance of respectability.

"Alice – at last!" Albert took her hands and gently pressed them to his own. Standing back, he studied her and frowned, "You look different."

"Oh? It must be my hair," she touched the loose curls gently. "I had a fringe cut."

"I dare say I shall get used to it."

Alice took his hand and gazed up into his face. He really did look very smart and she appreciated the effort he had made, knowing that working as a fitter in the engineering works was a dirty job.

"Mother and Father are waiting; the tea is in the pot."

Albert shook Reverend Tibbs' hand with enthusiasm and kissed her mother's slender hand, then seated himself in his usual seat. He had been taking afternoon tea here for the past six months. Mrs Tibbs poured his tea, passed him dainty sandwiches and scones, and fussed over whether he had enough jam for the scones and sugar in his tea. While buttering her own scone, Alice felt that her mother had taken over her own role in caring for Albert.

"Some apple cake, Albert?" Alice tried to fulfil

her role as future wife.

"No, thank you Alice, I've had plenty."

It all seemed rather formal. So very polite. But of course these were the ways of well-mannered people; how unreasonable to think of and long for the less polished ways she had become used to. No, this was just as it should be. If only Mother would allow her to pour Albert's tea and not take over so. He was very handsome and polite as always but it didn't quite feel as if he were hers.

"One of my colleagues is due for retirement and will be returning to be near family in Devon," Albert announced. "He has a company house on the green at New Town and thinks I've got a good chance of securing it when he leaves. I've been working there for eleven years now, since I was fourteen." He paused and smiled at Alice, "...and now I'm getting married in the summer. There is every chance that we'll have a new home for when we are together. What do you think of that, Alice?"

"It will be very convenient for work," Alice commented, trying to visualise the small development of terraced cottages and flats for the workers.

"A house, you say?" Reverend Tibbs looked up from his cake, "There are several blocks of flats I believe, decent, solid buildings."

"Yes sir, it is definitely a house. Two bedrooms and its own back yard. They may be forty years old but the railway took a pride in those houses when they built them; they are highly regarded as being quality homes. They are known as Dutch Gable houses, due to the Dutch influence in their style. Imagine that, Alice, our own house!"

It would be small, Alice reflected. Probably quite small compared to the vicarage, and even the schoolhouse which had generous rooms... and lacking the open space surrounding it. A yard, he said. A garden would be lovely with a flowering apple tree and a small vegetable plot. But, a home of their own, that would be very fine indeed.

"It sounds lovely, Albert. Perhaps we could take a walk around the area and see where the house is. Do you know which one it is?"

"I don't know exactly but I believe most of the homes face a green and it is an inner terrace; the end of terrace have three bedrooms." Albert replied. "A walk around the area is a splendid idea; shall we say tomorrow afternoon? Mother would love to see you, so perhaps we'll take a walk then after that back home to mine for afternoon tea?"

"That's a wonderful idea, Albert. How is your mother?"

The following afternoon found Albert at the front door of the rectory at half-past one. The day was overcast and threatened rain, which bothered Albert and he fussed as to whether the trip should be postponed.

"I have no intention of allowing the weather to put a stop to our outing," Alice told him. "If we waited for a fine day, we should never go anywhere or do anything at Dungeness. It's right on the coast, as you know, and there is rarely a day without a strong wind. The misty rain is miserable, it looks like nothing much but soaks through my clothes in no time and is quite depressing."

"Very well, but we must take an umbrella and make haste to get there before it rains." Albert offered Alice his arm as they set off down the path. "You seem to enjoy making it sound dreadful but I am sure you stay quite dry under an umbrella at Dungeness."

"I can't imagine ever being able to use an umbrella," said Alice who was feeling quite invigorated by the memories of the windswept point. "I am sure it would be blown apart in seconds."

"You do seem to be a little more forceful than I remember!" Albert remarked, "It must be all those children you have to keep in order."

"Oh, I hadn't thought... but of course they can be a little unruly." Alice resolved to be a little less outspoken as the couple walked along the lane towards the railway tracks. At the crossing they paused for an elderly man to shuffle out from his cottage, check the line was clear and allow them to cross. The rain clouds decided not to linger over Ashford and revealed a clear blue sky. It was a lovely day for a walk on a winter's afternoon.

In no time at all they reached the outskirts of Newtown, to their right the brown brick buildings of the South Eastern Railway Company workshops dominated the scene. Today they stood silent but six days a week the noise of the machinery filled the air, along with the smells of heated metal and smoke from the workshops. The clock tower at the entrance stood proud. The young couple turned their attention to the left and a development surrounding a large triangular green. It looked as if it had been styled on a traditional village but lacking the variety in age of properties. Young boys played a game of cricket on the grass while other children played with hoops nearby.

An elegant, brown brick building with six pillars rising up high above the first floor windows stood facing the green. Tall, ornate windows with curved tops gave decoration to the first floor and a row of shorter second floor windows, matched those below. The building boasted an Italianate style, used by the South

163

Eastern Railway Company and now reflected in its buildings for the workers.

"The public baths," announced Albert. "Eleven baths in there. Open Thursday, Friday and Saturday. Ladies in the morning, gents in the afternoons. I've taken to going there myself on a Saturday afternoon!"

"It's a beautiful building," Alice said with appreciation. She turned her attention to the building to the right of the baths. "Look Albert, a shop. Small but useful I am sure. What a shame it is a Sunday and we can't take a look inside. Perhaps Mother and I will take a stroll this way during the week."

"If you were to walk towards the railway works, there is a library, reading rooms and mechanics' institute. I imagine you would like the library and you might like to look in there with your mother."

"I'd like that, thank you, Albert."

"There's the pub, The Locomotive," Albert pointed to the left of the baths. "Closed today of course, but many of the workers go there for a pint after work or in the evening. In fact it even opens before six in the morning for the workers to start the day with an ale or porter." He reflected on this for a moment before adding, "but, of course, I won't get into that type of habit."

Alice nodded, but without understanding, as she had never been in a public house before.

On either side of the baths, shop and pub, making up one part of the triangular development were the rows of plain, flat-fronted, two storey flats. They were set back from the path with a small area of grass and shrubs in front of them. Again they were in the brown brick that seemed to be the theme for the area.

"Decent flats," commented Albert, "But as an

engineer I can hope for a house. My wages will easily cover the extra rent and the company pay both the rates and taxes."

With the bath house and flats dominating one side of the triangular green, the other two sides proudly displayed terraced rows of houses. Each terrace consisted of six houses with the houses at each end clearly being larger. Their decorative gable ends faced the road, showing an additional room in the taller roof height. Tall chimneys in sets of eight graced the roofs

"Oh Albert, what pretty houses. Look how trees have been planted amongst the terraces. I wonder which will be ours." Alice began to stroll across the green.

"I'll ask Mr Baldwin on Monday, then you can picture where it will be, on which side of the green."

Alice was now looking at the details, wondering what was behind the wooden doors with decorative glass inserts. What would her life be like living here with Albert?

"A parlour at the front, then the kitchen and a small lean-to scullery, I imagine." Albert stood, hands behind his back, looking up at the houses. "I wonder if there are flushing lavatories upstairs!"

"Wonderful," Alice said with enthusiasm, thinking of the miserable earth closet at Dungeness.

"I hear they have gas, they don't always you know, not workers' cottages," Albert continued. "Although I would say these are houses not cottages, wouldn't you agree?"

"Definitely," Alice happily confirmed.

"Do you see the gas street lamps?" Albert pointed to one. "A lamp-lighter comes around every evening and I hear the engine drivers appreciate them when they have to get up so early in the morning."

They were nearing the houses now and Alice noticed an unusual feature. "Look Albert, do you see that some of the gateposts are painted white? I wonder why."

"Now Alice, I can tell you about them. You can always tell an engine driver's home by its white posts. It's so the call boy knows which houses to knock at to wake them early!" Albert led them back to the corner of the green they had first come in at. "Now if we go around here, we can see the allotments."

They walked behind the terraced houses, noting the small yards, but perhaps that didn't matter with the trees on the green. Alice looked past the allotments, where several men were working, towards the water meadows and then the railway tracks. Albert was looking at the houses and soon Alice's attention was back on their future home.

"Imagine, Albert, if we lived here looking towards the fields at the back and to the green at the front. Both views are equally pleasant."

"Yes, as you say, it really is very pleasant. With both our savings, we'll be able to buy all the furniture we need, but I imagine the range and some of the fixtures will be ready waiting for us. We could redecorate if necessary."

"Perhaps when I return at Easter-time we could take a walk into town and look at the furniture shops? Imagine choosing all our own curtains and wallpapers and not having ones that someone else has used before." Alice gave Albert's hand a squeeze.

"We'll do that on a Saturday afternoon and have tea in the corner shop. That will be a treat! By then we'll know exactly which house it is and have another stroll around here."

"It sounds perfect, Albert. See how quickly we walked here from the rectory and your mother is only another five minutes away." Alice was beginning to picture it all and the future seemed very attractive. "How long would you say it will take to walk into the town? Perhaps twenty-five minutes?"

"Twenty-five minutes or perhaps half an hour. That sounds fair enough," Albert replied.

They had walked around the back of the houses which faced the green and Alice's attention was now drawn to another building, one which stood out from its brown brick neighbours. This was a Gothic style building of ragstone, which initially looked like a church with tall lancet windows and a high gabled bell-cote. Low boundary walls were topped with iron railings. It must be the school and so it drew her attention, she wanted to compare its size and grandeur to the one at Dungeness.

"Look Albert, the school. It's larger than our one at Dungeness, for we only have the one classroom. It does look like a nice school, rather grand though, don't you think? It's a town school so of course it will be bigger, but mine at Dungeness is a very good building too."

"Yes, the school for the railway workers' children. I am sure it is excellent."

As they neared the building Alice could read its name on a sign: "Newtown Railway School. And look, Albert, see the school motto here on a sign: 'Let cheerfulness abound with industry'. How suitable!"

"Very apt," Albert approved.

Alice thought of being in that little cottage all day, waiting for Albert to come home from the engineering works. Then she thought of her school and how lively the days were with the children, bright

167

and eager to learn.

"Albert do you thin ... how would it be if I were to, if I were to seek a teaching job? Perhaps just for the mornings?"

Albert turned and looked down at her for a few seconds, "Alice, how kind you are to think of those children and how you might be able to nurture those young minds, but we can't have people thinking that I can't support my own wife. That wouldn't do at all."

They turned, all interest in the school crushed, and walked back towards Albert's home for afternoon tea.

Christmas was over; the new year came with bright blue skies and clear starlit nights. The ground was hard with crisp white frosts every morning. Alice's parents took her in the trap to Ashford station on Saturday 5ᵗʰ January; the train was to leave at half-past twelve and they expected Albert to be there to see her off on the train. He was already at the entrance as they arrived and as Alice stepped down Albert took her hands.

"I shall look forward to your letters and when you come again it will be spring. We'll walk along to see where our home is to be."

"And to the town to look in the furniture shops," Alice added.

"Of course. I will be due a few days off work, so how does a day out in Hythe or Canterbury sound to you?"

"Wonderful," Alice smiled up at him. Until this moment she had accepted her return to Dungeness, but now she felt there was so much to miss out on here in Ashford, but also so much to look forward to on her return at Easter-time.

Chapter Eighteen
1895

As the train slowed down and eased itself into Lydd Town Station, Alice looked out, eager to see if she recognised anyone on the platform. She was pleased to spot the auburn hair and slim figure of Emily Brooks alongside the sturdier Connie Webb. Both women were well wrapped up and clutching at their shawls; the wind was so strong that Alice could feel the force of it pushing on the coach and thrusting its way through the window frames.

"Lydd, Lydd, all alight for Lydd. This train goes through to Dungeness." The station master, held onto his hat and did his very best to uphold his important position, but his words were whipped away on the wind and Alice only saw his lips moving from the relative comfort of the coach.

As Connie opened the door it was pulled from her hand, smashing against the side of the coach and back again towards the women. A young porter ran over and held it steady whilst the two women stepped up into the coach. They both smiled when they saw Alice and sat down opposite her.

"We were just saying that maybe you'd be back on this train after your Christmas holidays," Connie said.

"It's marvellous to see you." A warm feeling of

belonging settled in Alice's stomach. "Mrs Brooks... Emily, you look so much better, despite the cold."

Emily's skin and eyes glowed, having lost the shadows around her eyes and the haunted look within them. There was colour in her cheeks, so the difference between pale skin and red hair was not so stark. When she spoke, it was with a confidence Alice had not heard before:

"I've moved back round to Denge, back with Ed and we got married on the 29th December, last Saturday, just the two of us with Ben and Connie, and Tom Barton, he came too. He's been very good to Ed, really helpful."

"That's wonderful. Congratulations. I'm so pleased for you." Alice felt herself relaxing; 'Dungeness Alice' was back. A young woman who could like Emily and Ed for who they were and not judge them for living in sin the past year or more.

"Their Jake has gone," Connie informed. "Just went one day with not a word to his wife and family. His Helen was that upset, being left with three young children. They packed up before Christmas and left with just what they could carry."

"Where did they go?" Alice asked, trying to mask her horror.

"Over Camber way, she's got her family there." Connie leant forward to share her opinions, "A nasty man if ever there was. I'm sorry Emily, what with him being family but you know what I mean; your Edward is better off without that cousin of his."

"You're right Connie, I never liked him much, but family is family and he was all we had. Ed wonders if he had another woman somewhere and his Helen said as much." Emily looked at Alice and coloured a little. "Oh Miss Tibbs, I'm sorry... what with you being a vicar's daughter. I let my tongue run away with itself, I..."

"Don't you worry about that, Emily," Connie patted her arm gently. "Miss Tibbs sees all types here at Dungeness, she's used to our ways."

Alice was thinking about the situation the Brooks family were now in with fishing to be done and only the one man left who was fit enough to handle the boat. If life was tough for Ed Brooks before, how could he manage to support his wife and parents now? She had managed to push aside all thoughts of the accident while in Ashford and filled her mind with houses and Christmas festivities. How would she cope now back where the frightful incident happened? Could her teaching keep her busy enough to push those bad memories aside?

"How is Ed managing?" Alice asked tentatively. "With the boat?"

"He's got his father," Emily replied. "He always helps a bit but Ed doesn't like to push him too much, not at his age. But it's been wonderful, really it has, listen to this: Mr Barton, Tom I call him now, and Ben, well they have arranged some help for Ed. We've got Bert. You know Mrs Stevens from the lighthouse, he's her brother-in-law. And there's Will too, he's a young lad, but he's another pair of hands and Ed says he'll be all right once he's learnt the ropes."

So that was how the two young men had eased their guilt over the death of Jake Brooks. Not that it had been any more than an unfortunate accident, but they had seen the problems it would cause to his cousin. Ed Brooks couldn't manage without another strong man to assist him and the Dungeness neighbours had managed to help without looking as if charity was being given. Alice was

171

pleased that they were still doing their best to give support to the Brooks family.

"So Jake going hasn't caused any real problems for Ed and Emily, not now they've got more people looking out for them," Connie summed it up. "And good news for Emily today, you tell her Em."

Emily coloured a little, "I've been and got myself a job; that's what Connie and I were doing in Lydd. Just three days a week helping out in the bakery. I leave on the early train and they say it's fine if I come back on the twelve minutes past two, so even in the winter I'll be back before nightfall."

"That's fine news, Emily. Life is certainly getting better for you and Ed."

"I'm going to save up for a range. We've decided, Ed an' me, that it will make life much more comfortable."

"It will make your home far more pleasant," Alice agreed. "You'll have no need to worry if you step out for a bit as the fire will be perfectly safe and always ready for you when you need it."

The train slowed and the three women gathered up their belongings. Connie held the door as Alice struggled with her suitcase. Stepping down onto the platform, Alice was greeted by the full force of the wind coming straight off the sea. It took her aback for an instant and she felt that it was only the heavy suitcase that kept her weighted to the ground. She stepped into the station building, a temporary reprieve while she gathered up her back-stays before setting off to the schoolhouse.

The sea mists stayed clear of the headland for the next few weeks but the wind did not and with it came a chill that had surely come straight from the Arctic

Circle. The sky was generally clear and any clouds scurried along way up high. With no trees or substantial buildings to soften the impact of the icy winds, the residents of Dungeness moved from place to place with their long coats pulled tight around them, hats tied on and heads down. At night the sky was clear and the stars shone bright; by morning a hard frost lay over the shingle and low lying scrub-land.

School pupils arrived with pink cheeks and glowing eyes, exhilarated by their race across the shingle. Once in school their frozen fingers stung as they thawed in front of the fire. Coal was delivered regularly to the school, having come by train, and the two fires now burned in the school-room but still the staff and pupils were bitterly cold.

From four o'clock in the afternoon until the arrival of Mrs Stubbs in the early morning, Hazel and Alice sat close to the range in their armchairs, or under piles of blankets in their beds, with only each other for company. They felt like a pair of hermits as neither was inclined to set off in the darkness to visit family and friends in the village, and in return no one visited them in the evenings. Most Saturdays the young women set off on the morning train to Lydd, sometimes with Ruth or other local woman.

The sparse trees and solid buildings in the town gave limited protection from the wind, but generally it forced its way through the streets and there was no reprieve from the icy weather. However, it was a change of scene and they all enjoyed looking in the shops and spending a shilling or two on something to give them pleasure, such as a book or piece of jewellery, as well as the essential goods.

It was early February when Ruth arrived one morning having walked in from her home. As daughter

173

of a lighthouse keeper she lived in one of the houses circling the base of the lighthouse. She joined Mrs Stubbs, Alice and Hazel for a cup of tea before the day's work began.

"Your Ma came to mine with a message last night," Ruth told Hazel. "She was hoping you would join them for your sister's birthday this Wednesday evening. You too Miss Tibbs."

"Thank you, Ruth." Hazel replied as she poured the tea. "I can't miss Annie's birthday, even if it does mean stepping out in the cold."

"How kind of them to think of me," Alice was suddenly thrilled to have an excuse to break the monotonous routine imposed on them by the weather. "I don't mind a bit how cold it is; it will do us good to have some company of an evening."

"It can't stay cold like this for much longer and the days are becoming longer," Mrs Stubbs commented.

"Then we'll have the mists back and we'll be sorry!" Ruth laughed.

Wednesday came and after school Alice and Hazel changed from their plain black dresses into less formal clothes of softer shades. For Hazel it was her favourite mid-grey dress with a tiny floral repeat pattern and a pretty white crocheted collar. Alice wore her brown tweed skirt with a neat cream blouse, its pin-tucks had been ironed thoroughly the evening before.

Hazel insisted that Alice's new fringe was to be twisted around rags for an hour, and so her face would be framed by curls for the evening. Her own fair hair was plaited before being coiled at the nape of her neck. Together they chose favourite brooches and hair-clips.

174

At half-past five the friends pushed their boots into back-stays and slid off over the stones. They followed a wide track leading from the school in a north-easterly direction towards the Pilot. After a while they left the track and headed towards the cluster of cottages on the coast.

Back in the Ashford Rectory, the dining table had extra leaves that could be inserted and chairs that were taken from the corners of the room. Visiting children were seated separately, in the kitchen, to eat. No adult would be invited to dine if there were not a seat and table space for them; dining with or without guests was a formal occasion and good manners were paramount. So when Alice entered the cottage of Mr and Mrs Tanner and family, she was both shocked at the informal arrangements and admiring of the warm and friendly atmosphere that enveloped her.

The comfy chairs has been pushed to the edges of the room and a couple of elderly folk had claimed them. The two small children played and a baby lay at their feet. The usual dining table had been turned and another, presumably borrowed, was being butted up against it.

"This way a bit, Ben... no... yes, that's it. All lined up good and proper." Mr Tanner was at one end and Ben Webb the other. "That will do us nicely, put your chairs up that end."

"A couple more chairs?" Ben asked.

"If you wouldn't mind," Mr Tanner replied. "Now Hazel, my darling, lovely to see you. And you Miss Tibbs. Table cloths are on the side, Ma wants it all looking nice."

Mrs Tanner was busy at the stove. "Good to see you both; nasty weather out there but our Annie will be pleased you came along. Now Miss Tibbs, that's my mother and my husband's father sitting over there. The three little ones are my Annie's, her and Stan have just gone along to the Pilot for a couple of jugs of ale."

"The food smells delicious," Alice commented as she helped Hazel straighten the table cloth and then add an overlay of lace.

"You can't go wrong with a nice bit of rabbit this time of year," Mrs Tanner replied. With rabbits running freely over the area, it was a free source of meat. They couldn't burrow into the ground but had adapted to living amongst the roots of the broom and gorse.

As the cutlery and plates were placed on the table, Mr Tanner and Ben returned accompanied by Hazel's brother, Will.

"Connie is just on her way," Ben said. "She was wrapping up the pound cake and I put the jelly on the bench outside, Connie says it will melt if we have it in here in the warm."

"She's a good help," Mrs Tanner spoke with affection.

There was a fair volume of chatter in the room so no-one heard the sound of running footsteps on the shingle. No-one sensed the party was over before it had began. Unbeknown to them, a ship was in danger on the icy sea and had just sent up a flare. It was Stan and Annie on their return from the pub who spotted it and alerted the others.

"Pa, Ben, there's a flare out to sea, out to the east. Get your gear on." Stan hurriedly put the jugs of ale on the dresser. "Our Annie, she's gone to knock for the others."

The words were barely spoken before Ben was gone, letting the door slam behind him. Mr Tanner and his son were pushing past the extra table and chairs, going through to the front porch to get into their weatherproof jackets and boots.

Then to Alice's surprise the rabbit stew was taken off the range and Mrs Tanner was pulling on a long coat and fastening on her woollen hat. "Hazel, get the blankets warming by the range, will you, love." And with that she had also fled into the starlit night.

"Your mother, where's she gone?" Alice was unnerved by the reaction to the news of the flare.

"Out to launch the boat," said Hazel before leaving the room, presumably for the blankets.

"Launch the boat?" Alice repeated as Hazel returned.

"Come on, I'll show you." Hazel put down the blankets and spoke to her grandparents, "I'm taking Alice out to see the boat; you'll be fine with the little ones and Annie will be back in a moment."

"Take care, girls," her grandmother replied.

Coats and shawls were hastily put back on and the friends left through the back door. Their skirts were pulled up away from their ankles to enable them to run freely over the ridge and down to the beach. As they ran, other unrecognisable figures came from all directions to gather at the boathouse. That night it was the R.A.O.B lifeboat being sent to the rescue. Having just arrived in October, it was her first call out.

Alice and Hazel held back from looking in the boathouse. To get in the way would be unforgivable as the men fastened their life jackets in place and pulled on woollen hats. But it was what was happening on the shingle bank leading down to the icy sea that interested Alice: heavy planks of oak with ropes fixed to each end were being hauled into place by pairs of women.

"Those are the 'skids', the planks, I mean,"

177

Hazel informed. "We can't just leave them there, not with the shingle moving all the time, so it's up to the lady launchers to get them in place. We can't spare the men you see."

They watched in silence for a few minutes and it wasn't long before the R.A.O.B was coming out of the shed on its cart. It gathered speed as it moved down the bank and as it launched into the sea, it was the lady launchers who took the brunt of the bitterly cold water spraying out either side of the boat. This was going to be challenging enough for their men without heading off into the night already wet through. The launchers hauled the cart out of the water and returned to dry themselves off.

Standing there on the beach, Alice couldn't imagine how the lifeboat men could bear to be out with the bitterly cold wind that would find a way to sneak through the multiple layers of clothes and pierce a man's skin with its vicious energy. As the tide receded, ice was forming on the beach, yet for her and the lady launchers, a warm fire was only minutes away. The lifeboat could be out for hours. Alice felt her respect for these tough lifeboat men growing.

Supper was a subdued occasion. The rich rabbit stew spooned on crisp jacket potatoes was followed by a choice of pound cake or jelly. Conversation was polite and muted as all thoughts were on their men, Mr Tanner, Stan and Ben, who were out in this perishing cold weather. Alice wondered about the boat that was in danger, where was it heading? What was its cargo? Did it have passengers? Quietly, they prayed for both the lifeboat crew as well as the passengers and crew of the unknown vessel. Only the chatter of the toddlers kept the birthday meal from being eaten in total silence.

Then the call came: the lifeboat had been sighted and the land crew was needed. Lady launchers and blanket bearers pulled on coats and hats before racing back to the beach. Alice followed in the wake of Hazel's family, eager for news from the lifeboat. They were still at the top of the steep pebble beach when a call came from someone by the water:

"Man overboard, to the west. Man overboard."

Chapter Nineteen

Shouts carried on the wind to the watchers on the shore. But to Alice, standing on the bank with blankets in her arms, the voices were disjointed. Although the women were ready to catch a rope from the boat, then attach it to the capstan, the lifeboat crew were doing their best to hold the R.A.O.B steady just out from the shore. Ten pairs of oars tried to control it against the rolling waves whilst someone tried numerous times to throw a rope to the man in the water. All the shore crew could do was wait and try not to panic. Whoever had plunged into the water was a son to one of them, a brother to another and a cousin to several.

The pools of water left behind by the tide were frozen and it was clear that no one could last in the water for long. Their heavy clothes would be sodden and they would be exhausted after a couple of hours at sea. A lifeboat jacket would keep them afloat but the tide was retreating and the Dungeness currents were strong.

Then the moonlight revealed someone launching themselves into the sea with a safety rope attached to their waist. Within a few minutes those on land were horrified to see the lifeboat had given the signal that it was to be brought in and the rope now hung loose at its side. The land crew had to occupy themselves with the recovery of the vessel, moving the skids up the bank as the boat came in. They had to concentrate on the task at hand, to not let their fears affect their work. Shards of ice fell from the boat, glistened in the moonlight and smashed on the beach.

Then as the bow came clear of the water, a great cheer from those on the R.A.O.B and those on land saw that coming from the sea were the two men, one being carried by the other who had saved his life. A man jumped from the lifeboat and ran to relieve his crew mate of the heavy burden and, with the stones rolling under his feet, he staggered clear of the water.

Several of the watching women ran to the water's edge and it was Annie who first screamed out:

"It's Stan, it's Stan. Please God, don't let him be..."

"He's breathing," announced the exhausted crew mate as he laid him down on the stones. "You, Annie, stop your crying and get him out of this wet jacket, we've got to get him warm."

The other women backed away; they had a duty to the other crew members and whoever had been saved. Annie tended to her husband, with the help of Hazel. Alice, still cradling dry blankets, turned to the man sitting hunched on the beach. His crew-mate was with him pulling at the life-jacket.

It was then that Alice saw that the man who had launched himself into the freezing sea to rescue Stan was Tom Barton. She turned and knelt beside him and without asking for approval she began to peel his ice encrusted gloves from stiff fingers. Then, with her companion, she tackled his coat, undoing the fastenings and pulling him free of it. As it moved, more ice fell on the shingle and the sea-drenched layer was removed with no help from its owner who was now shaking violently.

Alice draped a blanket around Tom's shoulders

and rubbed his cold hands but he began to shudder regardless of her efforts. The other crew member was cold and wet too; they both needed to be moved off the beach and to have their wet clothes replaced with dry ones.

"Mr Barton, Tom, you've got to stand up, to get into the warm." Alice pulled at his sleeve and spoke to the other man. "And you too, you both need to get out of this wind."

Tom slowly stood, still shivering and wordlessly he began to put one foot in front of another while being guided up the bank. A man came running towards them and took the burden from Alice.

"Come on son, back to ours, your Ma has got it nice and warm and we'll have you fit in no time." Then turning to Alice he said, "Miss Tibbs isn't it? I hardly recognised you out here on the beach. You've helped keep him warm, thank you."

"Did everyone else get back safely?" Alice asked.

"Our men are all accounted for," the man replied. "We've four men rescued, but I can't say if we got them all. We'll find out soon enough."

They were at the top of the bank now and a stretcher came by with Stan on it. "He's conscious," Hazel called out. "Just that cold he can't do a thing for himself."

Alice was now concerned about the crew member who had come to take Stan from Tom's arms. He had waded into the sea and was already wet from being on the boat. He had done his bit and needed to take care of himself now. She turned to him and said, "Let me help with Mr Barton, you're cold through, please go and get warm yourself." The man nodded his thanks and turned towards the lifeboat house.

Now the lifeboat was slowly being winched up the beach. Alice learned later that the process could take a couple of hours. Local coastguards and young men who were not yet on the lifeboat crew took charge of the boat now. The winch, or windlass as they called it, was a wooden wheel with four handles extending out and it was these that were pushed around and around in order to pull the boat up the steep bank.

Alice knew there was plenty of help for the crew and the rescued. The best she could do was to enable Tom to get into the warmth of his parents' home. The three of them paused by a wooden cottage and the elder Mr Barton opened the door; Alice hung back, unsure of herself.

"Some help with his boots would be good," Tom's father said, and so Alice stepped in with them.

Tom slumped in an easy chair with the blanket wrapped tight around him. Alice's fingers, stiff with cold, fumbled with the laces and, as fingers began to thaw, the stinging sensation was unbearable. The boots had to be removed though and finally the first lace came loose and she was able to pull off a boot and thick knitted sock.

While Alice worked in silence, Tom's father spoke quiet words of reassurance as stubby fingers laboured on the next lace. As Alice rubbed the first foot with a corner of the blanket, his father finally worked the second boot loose. "There we are my lad, we can get those feet dry in no time. Miss Tibbs here, she's doing a great job." Then to Alice, "I'll get his top off, and you carry on rubbing his feet."

As the warmth gradually returned, Alice wondered about how many other women were doing this very same thing in the neighbouring cottages.

There was all the crew and those they had rescued, all of whom would need slowly warming. She concentrated on drying his feet and lower legs, keeping her eyes firmly away from the muscular upper body that was gradually being revealed as wet layers were peeled off. As the blanket was again wrapped around Tom, the door opened and his mother entered.

"I came as quick as I could but I saw Tom was safe, and it's so cold out there that many are in a bad way."

"He's doing all right," her husband replied. "He was shivering something chronic but it's easing now."

"Need to get those trousers off now; I've not done that in a long while," Mrs Barton smiled down at Alice who was still sitting at Tom's feet.

Time for Alice to move on, perhaps back to the Tanner household to check on Stan. But Mrs Barton saw her obvious discomfort and had another suggestion. "The kettle's on the range. I'm sure a cup of tea would help warm him through."

"Of course," Alice replied and moved out of the way so Tom's mother could take her place. "Do you have any news of the others?"

"It's the cold that's got them tonight. I'm sure the others will be fine, but I can't say for Stan, he was in the water for perhaps five or ten minutes longer than Tom. He's a strong lad though, hopefully he'll pull through."

Alice poured three cups of strong tea, stirred in sugar and set them on the table.

"You'll stay for tea, won't you?" Mrs Barton asked.

"I think I had better check on Stan and Mr Tanner and then... then I don't want to get in the way... so I'll go back to the schoolhouse." Alice was unsure of what was best, "That is unless I am needed elsewhere."

"I can see you are worried about your friends, so how about you pop in, then come back here and tell us how they are. Our Tom won't rest without news of Stan." Mrs Barton got up from her son's side. "I'll top up the pot and have a cup ready for you."

Alice wrapped her coat around her and again braved the chill night air. It took a moment for her to get her bearings and then she turned towards the Tanner cottage. On reaching the back door, Alice paused to knock, but then just opened the door and walked in.

The scene within the cottage was similar to the one she had just come from but three times as busy. Mr Tanner and Ben Webb sat side by side on the sofa, both wrapped in blankets over clean, dry clothes. On their laps were bowls of steaming rabbit stew. Hazel was pouring tea and Connie was stirring sugar in. Annie sat beside her husband who looked to be dozing.

"There you are; we were wondering where you had got to, but Hazel thought she had seen you helping with Tom," Mrs Tanner spoke, as she washed up the supper dishes. "Is he all right? He saved our Stan's life and risked his own; he's a brave man."

"I know; I saw him carrying Stan out of the sea. We didn't know it was Stan of course. They all looked the same until they got closer." Alice looked towards Stan and frowned a little, "Has he warmed through?"

"He seems to be fine," Annie replied. "He stopped shivering and managed to eat a little stew, then I gave him a brandy and he fell asleep, he was that exhausted."

"Well that's good to hear." Alice knew that Stan

couldn't have survived much longer in the icy water. She turned back to Mr Tanner and Ben, "Are you all warmed through?"

"We're fine," Mr Tanner replied while Ben nodded between mouthfuls of stew. "It was bad out there though; one of the worst."

"Cup of tea, Alice?" Hazel was about to pour.

"Oh no, I don't want to get in the way. Mrs Barton is making me a cup as I said I would let them know how Stan is, then I'll go back to the school. Thank you for the supper, Mrs Tanner and I'm sorry your birthday got spoiled, Annie. I'm just thankful the crew are safe."

Alice moved towards the door, saying her goodbyes and again stepped out into the cold. She suddenly realised how exhausted she was and would be thankful when she was finally sinking into her own bed. A few steps and she was knocking on the Barton's door before entering.

She found Tom sitting up, a cup cradled between his hands. He turned as Alice stepped into the room and gave a weak smile. His sister, Lucie, had now joined the family group and was sitting beside him.

"How's Stan?" Tom asked.

"He's fine, sleeping now in the chair, but he's eaten a little and had a brandy."

"That's probably what sent him to sleep," Tom grinned.

"Sit down, Miss Tibbs." Mrs Barton was pouring the tea. "You know my daughter, Lucie, don't you? Now, Tom was just telling us they saved the four crew but not the captain."

"Not the captain, how very sad," Alice's thoughts were back in that wild, grey sea.

"He wouldn't leave. Went down with the ship," Mrs Barton reported. "Men can be that foolish over their ship, some sort of pride."

"He wouldn't leave?" Alice repeated, frowning in disbelief.

"That's right," Tom confirmed, "and it's not that unusual. I've known it happen before. The captain sometimes thinks it's his place to stay with the ship."

"Did he think he could save it?" Alice asked.

"No chance of that." Tom shifted a little in the chair, becoming less hunched as the tea warmed him. "No, it's just the way it is, perhaps he didn't want the humiliation of losing his vessel."

"So he lost his life," Alice reflected. "How very sad."

They talked for a few more minutes in a desultory way; Alice felt her limbs relaxing and her eyes beginning to close. She stifled a yawn.

"Time to get back," she said. The walk would be a long one tonight and the schoolhouse would feel especially remote.

"I'll walk you back," Mr Barton stood up.

"Thank you, but I'll call in for Hazel and we'll go together."

My dear Alice,

I had to put pen to paper to express my distress when I read about the lifeboat rescue. How very brave those men are but I can hardly credit that one was so careless as to fall overboard. What imagination you have in describing the 'lady launchers' I could almost believe it and marvellous of them to support the good men who launch the boats.

My love, I feel I must express my concerns. It wouldn't do to be repeating these tales back home in

Ashford. I am sure Mother would be most worried about you forming friendships with the women of the fishing families. Less said, as they say.

Here, I am waiting in anticipation for news that I have secured a home for us. My application is being reviewed and I can see no reason why we will not be successful.

I saw your parents last night but did not discuss the lifeboat incident, not wanting to distress them unduly.

I look forward to the spring and with it your return to Ashford in the school holidays.

With my fondest thoughts, Albert.

Alice put the letter in the soft leather pouch with her writing paper and stamps. She felt rather depressed and as much as she told herself that Albert had never been to Dungeness and couldn't understand what it was like, Alice couldn't shift the feeling that he was being unreasonable. Then she felt cross with herself for being unfair to Albert.

The freezing weather had passed, thankfully. February turned into March and with it came a return of the sea-mists, often lingering all day. Then, just as it seemed that spring would never arrive in this desolate corner of Kent, the mists became less frequent and there seemed to be a definite increase in the temperature. At times, when outside, Alice even felt a gentle warmth on her back and it gave her a feeling of contentment. But this was the Dungeness point on the Kent coast and the next gale was never far away.

Chapter Twenty

Alice woke with confusion. An almighty crash had descended into her idyllic dream where she and Tom, no Albert... of course it was Albert... were walking along the canal or was it a river? Well, it had all been very pleasant and sunny and they – they being her and Albert – had been holding hands and.... That was the trouble with dreams, so real for a moment and then they faded away and she was left trying to pick up the pieces and get back to sleep with confused thoughts in her head.

It was lovely and warm in the soft bed, but a distant creaking sound was niggling Alice. Not loud enough to be clear what is was, but enough to make her focus on it. All the time she was bothered by the persistent creak, she would never settle back to sleep. Whatever could the time be? It was still pitch black, but then it was still only March. Another crash, or more of a thud, came. Enough to make Alice think that should get out of her bed and investigate or she would never be able to settle.

She swung her legs out of the bed and felt for her slippers, then wrapped her woollen shawl tight around her shoulders. On opening her bedroom door, Alice jumped and her heart crashed about beneath her ribs; Hazel was standing there in her long white night-gown.

"You heard it too then," Hazel said. "Please

God it weren't one of the chimneys coming down. That happened to our nan a couple of years back and it made a terrible mess, it did."

"Oh, no," Alice considered it. "Just think of all the slates here on the schoolhouse, they would be all smashed and falling down to the ground in little pieces. It wouldn't be the one big crash and then nothing. I'm sure the front gate is open and swinging; we must have forgotten to tie it, but the crash... maybe out the back?"

"The hen-coop? We'd best look, although there's nothing to be done if the poor things have lost their home. Not now, not in the dead of night."

Alice had been living in Dungeness for nearly five months now and thought she had experienced all the types of bad weather that could possibly happen here. But on opening the back door, it was clear it was only the shelter of the solid schoolhouse stopping the wind from picking up the two young women and depositing them in Lydd or beyond. They stood at the corner of the building listening to the howl of the gale and the noise of debris scurrying along in the wind. Pieces of slate, wood and branches of gorse or broom knocked against the side of the building or were deposited on the shingle, often to be picked up again in the next squall. The moon was full, casting patchy light on the area, as clouds raced across its face. As they stood to take in the scene, a slate fell, missing Hazel by inches, causing her to clutch at Alice. They pressed themselves against the rough wall of the schoolhouse, partially protected by the overhanging eves.

"It's not safe to be out here." Alice, as teacher and with three years more experience of life, pulled Hazel back in through the doorway. "Did you see the privy, and how lopsided it was? Nothing we can do about it now though. We'll just have to take our chamber pots as far as we think right and empty them out in the morning."

"We'll go over to see Peggy's husband. He does the odd jobs out here on the school."

"Very well," Alice replied. "We can check with Mrs Stubbs and one of us can go to see him in the morning. Gosh, I'm cold, not surprising out there in our nightdresses. There's nothing more we can do until the gale eases. Let's try and get some more sleep."

They slept in fits and starts, bothered by the erratic creaking of the front gate and tense with fear of hearing another crash. When the very first weak light from the rising sun crept around their curtains, the young women were pleased to have an excuse to rise from their beds. They huddled in armchairs, bleary eyed, in front of the range and with mugs of hot chocolate in their hands. When the first noises of the steam train could be heard, crocheted blankets were discarded from their knees and the young women raced to get dressed before Mrs Stubbs arrived.

"I think we should be thankful if we have escaped with just a few slates lost and the privy all askew," Mrs Stubbs concluded. "Not that I am belittling the loss of a privy. Most inconvenient. Of course we must see if Mr Webb is available to make repairs and I am not inclined to wait for Peggy to take the message to him after dinner time. The wind has dropped so I suggest the pair of you hasten over to the village and call on Mr Webb. By all means check on your family, Hazel. Ruth and I can manage for an hour."

The wind had eased, although it was still a brisk south-easterly. Still low in the sky, the sun was deceptive, giving promise of a pleasant day, which could never be fulfilled. Alice and Hazel set off towards Dungeness village, heads bowed towards the wind but grateful its pace had slackened overnight. The landscape had always looked wild, but today it had an unkempt look about it. Severed branches of gorse and broom lay wilting, their pale flesh torn at the point where they had been ripped off their parent plant by the force of the gale. Wooden shingle roof tiles were strewn randomly on the ground; slivers of smashed slate lay in grey pools. Lone pieces of netting and tarpaulin moved listlessly in the wind.

All over the headland men and women could be seen alone or in pairs. Alice presumed the salvage work had begun. To see so many figures scattered over the area in this way was unusual, they usually kept to the village and beach. There they were, hauling bits of wood or a reluctant goat back towards their cottages. The children were busy too, caught up in the excitement of chasing after a chicken that had found its freedom or passing a tile to a father on a roof. A storm such as this came with an unwritten rule: A full day at school took second place to family duties.

"There's a few folk who have lost their goats and chickens overnight," Hazel commented. "It's always the way after a bad storm. We've got to gather them up as soon as we can."

They neared Mr and Mrs Webb's cottage to find Peggy putting a chicken back in its newly repaired pen.

"We'll not be gettin' any eggs from this lot for a while," was Peggy's comment as Alice and Hazel drew closer. "Now what brings you two here when you should be up over there at the school. Summat wrong?"

"Nothing much, Mrs Webb. It's just that the

privy fell down in the night," Alice began, "and Mrs Stubbs asked if Mr Webb could..."

"Come an' fix it? He's just out checkin' on the boat an' then he'll be along shortly. Been up since the crack of dawn, he has, fixin' the coop and now off to the boat."

"Wonderful, thank you."

"We'll see you later then, Peggy," Hazel said as they turned away.

"Smoked dabs for yer dinner." Peggy called after them.

The children knew to leave their disagreements behind them as they arrived at school in the morning and afternoon. Mrs Stubbs had no interest in childish tittle-tattle. However they sometimes found a sympathetic ear from Hazel or Ruth once the headteacher had left for the day. It was rare that an argument from the playground found its way to the school-room but that day they began to bicker as the lines of children entered the building.

"It's not fair, it's always him that does the tellin' an' it's my story. It were my pa that told his, so we knew first, not him." Young Dora's eyes brimmed with tears and her cheeks were flushed.

"Well, jus' get on and tell then, Dora, or he will. You know he will. Boys are like that, always wantin' to make trouble." Em, the youngest of five spoke from experience.

"Me Pa says there's a body, another body found out over Denge way," Fred raised his voice as he announced with glee. "It were a man this time, just lying there an' he aint newly dead neither."

"He did it, he told," squealed Dora and the tears flooded, whilst her girl friends gathered around, scowling at Fred.

Fred's face had the kind of superior smile you see on a child who has bettered another. He stood half a head taller than the little girl and was two years older than her. Two years' more life experience as well as having two big brothers who had excelled in their duty to train him to be annoying. He looked across at the little girl and said:

"You know I tell it better, Dora. It needs a man to tell about things like bodies and dyin', don't it?"

"I don't see no man here, Frederick Brown," laughed Victoria Stevens. "Jus' a silly little show-off."

Fred's brown eyes scowled at Victoria, eyebrows knitted together. "Well, I still told it first," were his final words.

"Enough," snapped Mrs Stubbs. "Frederick Brown, you know better than to come in here shouting your news. This is a school room not a street market. Dora, stop wiping your eyes with your apron, find a handkerchief and use it. All of you, back outside, line up sensibly and in silence. Now." Mrs Stubbs drew a deep breath and turned to Alice, "Miss Tibbs, call them in, if you please."

How she walked across the room to the doorway and called the children in, Alice never knew. She moved like some form of automated machine, following Mrs Stubbs' directions. She knew whose body had been found and strangely enough she felt relief. For three months Jake Brooks had lain in his shallow grave, inland from his home at Denge. A whole quarter of a year with no proper funeral service and without being laid to rest in the correct way. In all that time his wife and family assumed he had run off and abandoned them; they deserved to know the truth. Well, not the truth... but to know that he had not just gone without a care for them.

This man needed to have a proper burial service and perhaps then he could answer to God in heaven for his sins. It wasn't up to her... to her, Tom and Ben... to lay him to rest in unconsecrated ground, perhaps leaving his spirit forever in an in-between place between life and death. Alice hadn't really considered it before, she had refused to think of it, pushing him away from her thoughts if he ever threatened to prey upon them. Now she saw it very clearly; Jake Brooks must have a funeral service and be laid to rest in the proper way.

In the time that had passed, Thomas Barton and Ben Webb had gone out fishing, manned the lifeboats, made repairs to their homes and whatever else the men did. Alice had taught at the school, written her letters home and kept herself busy with daily chores. The three of them never mentioned the accident, for that was what it was. But how could they ever truly live their lives without guilt whilst a body lay covered beneath a thin layer of shingle just a short distance away? Even when she returned to Ashford her memories of Dungeness would be tarnished by the one terrible event.

"You've not got one of your headaches coming?" Hazel asked Alice as the school day ended. The children had gone and it was just the teacher and her assistants left to tidy up.

"A headache... I... well, just a slight one," Alice tried to pull herself into the present. "Nothing to worry about."

"It's just that you do look awfully pale, doesn't she, Ruth?"

"I expect Miss Tibbs is just tired after the storm last night," replied Ruth. "I know I am and you were both up in the night."

"Yes, that will be it." Alice snatched at the excuse. "I'll be fine in the morning."

"So we'll have a cup of tea and a currant bun then the three of us can go out and find out who it is. If it's even true, because there's no one gone missing from hereabouts and it don't... doesn't... sound like he's come from the sea, not if he was found all the way inland." Hazel led the way through to the schoolhouse.

"I hadn't thought," Alice began. "I hadn't thought we would be going out to find out who... who he is or was. Isn't it a family matter?"

"But we won't know whose family he is unless we go and find out, will we?" Hazel put tea leaves in the pot. "There's buns in the larder, if you don't mind, Ruth. I think Alice must have one of her headaches coming on so we'll sort out the tea shall we?"

Alice found herself caught up in it all and, for some reason that she couldn't quite fathom, she trailed after Hazel and Ruth. Across the tracks they went and towards the distant ribbon of curious onlookers who had been to see the body, and were now on the return journey. Trudging up and down the shingle banks to satisfy the curiosity of her companions, Alice went to face the dead man.

Why hadn't she just spoken up and said that it really wasn't her business? Whoever's family it was, it certainly wasn't hers. But of course she couldn't just settle down with a book and a cup of tea, because she had to know for absolute certain that it was his body uncovered by the storm.

Their destination was marked by a couple of old men, sat hunched up together, as sentinels for the

196

body. The body itself appeared to be covered with a blanket. The last of the spectators were now some distance away and the area had almost returned to its previous state of being quite desolate, having no properties nearby and nothing to offer either farmer or fisherman. It had been a good location to conceal a body, but not good enough.

The men looked up as they neared and one spoke:

"Come to pay yer respects have yer?"

"That's right, Bert," Hazel replied. "We thought we should, as soon as school ended. You're keeping an eye on him are you?"

"Tha's what the vicar said was right and proper. He's gone on the train to Lydd and most likely he'll bring the constable back wi' him. This being not a normal sort of death, if you see what I mean."

"A normal type of death?" Alice asked, her voice high and unnatural.

"Well, like a drowning or illness..." He paused to ponder on it, "or even a normal type of accident. No, when a body is just lyin' around and that body is a young man then it's not a normal type of death whatever way you see it."

"I see," Alice replied.

"We've come over to see who he is," Hazel informed. "I can't think, well none of us can, that it could be anyone from Dungeness."

"Ah, no it ain't no one from Dungeness but he's from hereabouts," Bert turned and nodded towards the figure. "It's that bad un from Denge, that Jake Brooks, him what was up t' no good."

"Oh gosh," replied Hazel. "They said he'd gone off and no one knew where."

"Well they do now," Bert replied, his companion

197

nodding in agreement.

"His wife left for Camber," Ruth said. "She'll have to be told."

"Of course she will, lass, an' no doubt the constable is on his way already." Bert paused to ponder on it for a moment and continued, "They'll bring a cart no doubt."

"A cart?" Alice repeated.

"I'm thinking of the body. Stands to reason that the vicar don't want no body rottin' away at his. Now newly dead is a different matter, they waits at the vicarage until the funeral. No, this one will be going straight to Lydd on a cart and no need for you girls to worry about it."

All the time they spoke, Alice could barely take her eyes off the blanketed body. She took a step closer and eyed its contours; the rough blue blanket had settled in nicely around him and at the corner it rose and fell gently with the breeze, revealing the heel of a black boot. Alongside the body and head, stones had been placed to keep the cover in place.

"You don't want t' see no dead body," said Bert, following her gaze.

"Oh no... no... I just. It's all very sad," Alice finished lamely.

"It's been that cold, it's kept him nice and shipshape," Bert informed. "Not that a damned sinner like him deserves to lie peaceful in a grave, but tha's up to the vicar and God to say."

"Of course it is," Hazel replied briskly. "No doubt the cart will be here soon and that will be the end of it. We'll be getting back now. We just had to see who it is, to be sure it wasn't anyone we knew, anyone from Dungeness."

"It will only be that Ed Brooks to shed a tear

over 'im, and he's been a changed man since that Tom Barton set him up with some decent men to work alongside him on the boat. He'll not waste much time worrying over that no good cousin of his, not if he has much sense about 'im. No, he might just say good riddance like the rest of us."

"I'm not sure about that Bert," Hazel replied as the three of them turned away. "But I've no doubt Ed knows he's better off without his cousin."

With that, the three young women retraced their steps over the undulating shingle and back towards the railway tracks. They didn't talk, two of them wondering why the body of that no-good Jake Brooks had been buried in a shallow, shingle grave a little inland of his Denge home. They hoped that it had nothing to do with any of the Dungeness villagers or his cousin Ed, who was fast becoming one of their own. Hazel and Ruth could never have imagined, as they glanced at Alice, that her thoughts were so much more turbulent than their own. Behind her calm gaze there was both fear of what might happen next and relief that the body had at last been revealed. At the railway tracks, they parted with a few brief words; Ruth turning towards the coast and her lighthouse keeper's cottage.

Alice and Hazel walked on in silence, soon reaching the picket fence surrounding the schoolhouse. As they paused at the fence, they saw in the distance, on the track that led directly from Lydd, a cart and three dark figures. They waited and watched, in silent agreement, the progress of the figures who soon revealed themselves as being the constable and the vicar, as well as a labourer who pushed the cart which would, on its return journey, carry the body.

Chapter Twenty-One

"Not going up to Lydd today then?" Peggy's sharp eyes were on Alice as she bustled in and placed her basket on the table.

"No, I had a few chores to do," Alice looked up from her darning. Was it that time already? She really hadn't wanted to face Peggy's scrutiny. She began to gather her patched up stockings. "It's a lovely day, I thought I would walk out to the sea. Who would have thought that we've just had that dreadful storm and now it is calmer than ever." She was talking too much, she knew that and must not give away any of her inner thoughts to that dreadful Mrs Webb.

"A lovely day for some," Peggy repeated darkly. She unwrapped skinned rabbit and slapped it down on the wooden table. "Not so nice for that wife of Jake Brooks. Poor woman has turned up here already, must have been walking since before dawn. Gone to see Ed and then the vicar, no doubt."

"Poor woman," Alice reflected on what it must be like to believe your husband had run off with another woman, only to learn that he'd not even made it as far as Lydd. She fastened her walking boots and gathered her shawl. "Thank you for preparing our dinner, Mrs Webb. I'll see you at church tomorrow."

Alice didn't follow the railway tracks towards the coast, but took the path that led towards the Pilot and the fishermen's cottages. It wasn't a path in the sense that it was much different from the ground around it, but the traffic from foot and carts kept it free from plants. Some of the younger children were out playing tag and ball games; she gave a wave but was determined not to linger. The older ones would be busy with chores; a mother needn't work the water pump if there was a strong worker to do the job for her.

It took at least twenty minutes to reach the cottages standing just back from the beach bank. Alice walked between the fishermen's homes, alongside the lifeboat house and stood on the ridge looking out to sea. The steely grey water, having lost much of its recent spirit, had slunk back as low as Alice had ever seen it. Waves rolled in, with a marked lack of enthusiasm, deposited very little in the way of debris and backed away pulling a little of the brown sand with them.

The band of sand was clean, but being so flat it remained too waterlogged to tempt Alice to walk along it. Instead she carefully side-stepped down the steep bank and walked along the base of it. There was no hurry and she often paused and stooped down to inspect an unusual shell or remains of a sea creature. Twice she pocketed a stone with a hole right through it and once discarded a holey stone as not being formed neatly enough. Hag-stones they were called by the locals who believed they had magic powers. For Alice they made an attractive decoration strung up by the back door of the schoolhouse. Maybe something to take home with her and remind her of her time in Dungeness.

From her position at the bottom of the shingle bank, Alice couldn't see the cottages or even the fishing boats which perched on top of it. As she gradually began her ascent, the bows of the boats appeared. They were all on the ridge, it being a Saturday, a day for relaxation and repairs. Several of the fishermen were there and nodded a greeting, but they left her to her walk. Alice spotted Tom Barton by his boat and as she passed by he called out a casual greeting:

"Good day, Miss Tibbs. A fine morning for a walk."

"It is. How thankful we all must be that the wind has eased." Polite words, covering a multitude of questions and thoughts that stormed around in her head. "Did you suffer any storm damage?"

"Just my net shed, it's taken a battering but I've been able to right it." He stepped closer and spoke quietly, "They found him then."

"He can be laid to rest now," Alice replied.

"His wife's over at Denge, with Ed and Emily. She'll stay for the funeral and then back off to Camber."

"The funeral... of course." Not in the school, please not in the school.

"It'll be in Lydd, Monday afternoon. Some of us are walking up and coming back on the train. Ben and I, we've got to go, to support Ed and Emily. Not that it will be easy of course."

"No, no it won't be." To go to the funeral of the man you've killed and already buried, to go there and give your last respects. Alice's stomach recoiled at the very thought of it; she wouldn't go. No, there was no need for that at all. "And has anyone been asking? The constable I mean... has he... has he spoken to anyone?"

"He's been along to see Ed and of course someone spoke to the wife last night. There's nothing to tell. Emily was over here with Connie, and Ed was in Lydd that day. He'll go over to Denge and see the old folk but they saw nothing. The constable will do his job, up to a point. Ask a few questions and go back to Lydd. He'll not be hanging around here longer than he has to."

"I see." But Alice didn't see how a body could be found in a shallow, shingle grave and once found, that it could be dealt with in such a casual manner. It wasn't the way it would be in Ashford; certainly there would be a proper enquiry and paperwork. Yes, there would be papers to write and forms to fill. But Alice didn't know, not really, exactly how it would be dealt with in Ashford because this was beyond the realms of her experience.

"I'll be seeing you then." Tom turned back to his work. It wasn't the place to be discussing the matter any further and both were satisfied the secret was safe between the three of them and the shingle grave.

Jake Brooks was buried at the expense of Lydd Parish on the Monday. Those who attended the funeral walked along the tracks, passing the school, and on to Lydd. From the high windows of the schoolroom, Alice didn't see them pass but her mind was on them, as they made their pilgrimage to pay their last respects, not to the dead man but to his wife and family. He had no one left at Denge now and even his cousin was working with the men from around the point at Dungeness.

Alice didn't want to hear of the funeral. Who had been there. What had been said. Although whether it was mentioned or not, the thoughts of the dead man filled her mind. Mrs Stubbs had no cause to discuss the service, but eventually it was Peggy Webb who felt the need to raise the subject, as the teachers and assistants ate salted cod from Peggy's own stores.

"He'll be in the earth by now," the old woman commented as she washed up large pans at the Belfast sink. "Jus' earth, no nice brick sides, not on the parish."

"No one here will shed a tear," Ruth replied.

"Denge or not, he brings shame on his family to be in a common grave," Peggy persisted.

"A penny a week for funeral insurance isn't always easy to come by," Mrs Stubbs replied calmly. "I'm sure his wife tried her best, but she has children to feed and clothe. She put her children first and I commend her for it. There's many a family who go without food or heat to pay for a respectable grave."

"She'll be back to Camber tonight and not looking back," Peggy snatched the plates away as soon as the last morsels were eaten.

"Lovely cod, Mrs Webb. Delicious." Mrs Stubbs closed the subject.

Later that afternoon, as Mrs Stubbs prepared to leave for the day, the unmistakable sound of the train rattling by reminded Alice that those who attended the funeral would be returning home now by the twelve minutes past two from Lydd. It was over.

Alice left with the fish on the early morning train to Lydd, the following Saturday. She had left Hazel a note, saying that she would meet her as the mid-morning train came into Lydd; she had a job to do, so was leaving early. Before her friend had risen, Alice was very quietly raising the latch and creeping off across the shingle. How she would explain herself, she had no idea, as sneaking off to Lydd at this early hour would seem most out of character.

The fish was being loaded as Alice reached the small station. Wooden crates were being passed into the luggage van and stacked, most likely ready for a journey to London. The south-westerly wind was brisk and so the fishermen had their hoods up and kept their eyes on the job. After a night at sea, they were intent on the task in hand and if any of them noticed the young teacher stepping into the coach, they were not inclined to comment on it.

In the early hours of the Saturday morning, Alice was the only passenger, for which she was thankful. With her shawl pulled tight around her shoulders, she huddled in her seat and gazed unseeing across the shingle ridges, looking on as they blended into flat farmland before eventually reaching the distant hills. Within ten minutes the scalloped canopies of the station buildings were clear to see and a couple of staff emerged. They stared at her, not expecting a passenger at this time, but Alice's serious face discouraged idle comments so she went on her way without any bother.

The station was a short walk from the main town and, once out of the yard, Alice walked briskly along Station Road. She gazed at the weather-boarded smock mill to her left and then with disinterest at the houses that emerged on either side of her as she neared the town centre. Nodding politely at people who passed her on the street, she could not have said if they were man or woman, young or old. It wasn't a day to be paying attention to the details.

Station Road, now flanked by terraced cottages, swung to the right then straightened again. Past the slumbering Star Pub and the ornate red brick Mission Hall, Alice walked and then, as the main road again bore to the right, she chose to ignore the deviation and continued straight ahead into Church Road. Only now that her goal was in sight did Alice's pace falter and she wondered about the wisdom of her outing. She slowed to admire the pretty cottages on either side, their low roofs of weathered red tiles, and plants creeping up rendered walls, giving promise of floral beauty in the coming months. For now, primroses and bluebells sat in clusters within the narrow band of earth between cottages and road. Then she studied the cottages with their upper storey clad in black weather-boarding and pondered whether she preferred the distinctive black or more traditional white boarding. Finally, before entering the churchyard, Alice paused to appreciate the substantial old house, set back a little from the road. She wondered what lay behind the fine square windows and smiled at the tiny dormers peeping from the red tile, hipped roof.

Now the road ended and there was nowhere else to go but to step through the gateway into the churchyard. She gazed up at the eastern end of the medieval church, liking the form of the traditional window with detailed stonework. Then looking to the tower on the far end, Alice wondered if, at some point during the day, the eight bells would ring with joy for all to hear in the small town.

It was to Alice's right, where the churchyard was bordered by a low brick wall, that the pile of freshly dug earth lay dark and moist in a gentle mound. She picked up her skirts so the hems were not soaked by the dew-laden grass and walked steadily towards the grave. There was no marker, as befitted a pauper's grave. The only signs of the recent ceremony being some bundles of evergreen leaves and wilted early spring blossom.

Alice stood beside the grave in silence for a minute or two, her head bowed and eyes fixed on the soft bare earth. Then she spoke, very quietly, without faltering:

"May God forgive you for your sins and he knows there were many. May he forgive me for allowing you to lie in a shingle grave. I will take the blame for nothing else. I leave you now, knowing that you have been buried as you should be and with the hope that you will repent in heaven. Dear God, I pray that this man's family; may they find peace and comfort in this harsh world and may his children live to be better men than their father." At this point Alice took a step from the grave and, before turning her back on Jake Brooks forever, she recited the Lord's prayer in the same level tone: "Our Father, which art in heaven, hallowed be thy name...."

In those few minutes Alice had stood at the graveside, it was as if only herself and the dead man existed. She had lost all sense of her surroundings and had no awareness of any other person being nearby. So, when she turned and saw someone stood just a few yards behind her she was momentarily stunned. It felt that all her inner thoughts and fears were laid bare for this stranger to read. She stood frozen, for a moment, her brown eyes fixed upon the grey ones of this other young woman.

Her hair was pale, bleached, as if life had drained all colour from it. It was pulled back in a small bun, flat behind small ears that stuck out a little. Her cheek-bones were prominent and her skin had no colour to it, nor any distinguishing marks. The large grey eyes, were the only sign that in another time, another life, this woman could be beautiful. As she stood, her long black skirt hung awkwardly as if it was meant for a larger woman and had been gathered in at the back. Thin, blue veined hands clutched at a ragged black shawl, pulling it tighter in a vain attempt to keep the woman warm.

"Did you know 'im?"

"I... no. No, I didn't, not at all."

"Jus' passin' by?"

"Just passing by," Alice confirmed. "I stopped and just spent a moment. Giving my respects."

"He don't deserve yer respects. He was a bad un, our Jake. I weren't sorry, not when he went off and not when they found 'im dead."

"Oh...I."

"I shouldn't say that, should I? Not to a lady like you." She paused, and frowned a little. "Have I seen you hereabouts before?"

"I've been staying at Dungeness, at the school."

"You're that new teacher. The one that helped Ed." She nodded as her dulled brain pieced together the memories. "That were good of you. He's all right, Ed is. I hope he gets a chance now with Jake gone."

"That's right, I helped Ed tidy up their home."

"So, now you're here. Jus' passing by and you stopped off to say a little prayer, even though you knew he was a bad 'un."

"It seemed like the right thing to do," Alice confirmed.

"Yes, I can see it would, what with you bein' a vicar's daughter or so I hear."

Alice took a step back from the widow. "I'll leave you to have a moment alone. I've some errands to do in town."

"Thank you. I'll have a word and then I'll be off

208

meself. Stayed overnight with me cousin; the constable wanted to see me but it's done now and I'll set off to Camber now, maybe get a lift if I'm lucky."

"Good bye then," Alice took a few steps back towards the church. Then feeling deep in her pocket she took a handful of coins and turning back she thrust them awkwardly at the stranger. "Here, take them. For the children."

"Ta. I don't like to take charity, but I can't say that the children don't need it."

Alice walked away neither looking back at the grave or the young widow. Hot buttered toast and a pot of tea at one of the local tearooms beckoned.

Chapter Twenty-Two

"Look Miss, a rainbow," young Dora tugged at Alice's sleeve. "Look Miss, it's going right over my house an' all the others."

Alice looked up and saw to the south-east a glowing arc, radiating from near the lighthouse. It shone vividly from red through to violet within a steel-blue sky, then faded a little as it brushed over low lying clouds above the sea, before reaching its final destination.

Alice didn't long for a pot of gold at the end of the rainbow; no that was for the likes of her namesake who visited Wonderland. Where this rainbow ended would suit her very nicely. She was sure, if only it were possible to reach it, that this rainbow ended in Hythe. Once in Hythe she would sit in a toast-rack tram carriage with Albert beside her, just like last summer, and be transported to the seafront. The sun would be warm on her skin and the sky a cerulean blue. They would stroll along the promenade and maybe have tea and cake at The Imperial. Then a walk along the military canal, pausing to admire the well-kept flower beds and standing on a bridge to look down on graceful swans. Yes, that would be her pot of gold at the end of the rainbow.

"Children, come here," Alice beckoned them and they stood in a semicircle around her. "Let us make our own rainbow, in our own colours from the stones we have here. It can go from charcoal and brown, through to pale grey, beige and white. Will we be able to find enough white stones do you think?"

She started organising them all into groups and the children soon caught her enthusiasm, eager to go searching beyond the boundaries of the school playground.

"Who's that walking under the rainbow," Eliza asked her friend, Dora.

Dora squinted into the distance, "I think it's Mr Barton. My ma thinks he's ever so handsome, but he's ever so old, maybe even thirty."

"What do you think, Miss Tibbs?" asked Dora.

"Don't be silly girls," Hazel interrupted, "Miss Tibbs has a special man friend back home in Ashford. Now come along, you're meant to be looking for whites, I'll help you."

It was Tom Barton striding out towards the school. By the time he reached the perimeter fence the rainbow had been completed and the children were lining up to go inside.

"'Ere Mr Barton," called Fred. "Did you know you walked under a rainbow? Have you come to see ours?"

The orderly line was broken as the younger pupils vied to be the ones to show their bit of the pebble picture. Alice allowed them a minute or so and then called out:

"Now then, back in your lines, boys behind Ruth, girls with Hazel. Quickly now." Then she looked at Tom enquiringly, "Was there something I could help you with? Or do you have a message for someone?"

"It was you I came to see," he looked down at her, grey eyes softly creased around the edges, dark blonde hair wildly curling in the wind. "I've some news,

211

but I'll wait whilst you see the children off." Then he sat himself down on the edge of a ridge, which served as a seat for the children at playtime. It was as if he had all the time in the world to wait and clearly wasn't going to tell Alice yet.

She turned back to the school and helped Ruth tidy up whilst Hazel read the class a chapter of Alice in Wonderland. Then, as the children raced home or walked along in small groups, according to their age, Alice went back out to the playground.

"You've something to tell me?" Alice asked.

"It's about my uncle," Tom continued to sit on the shingle bank, looking up at her. "He's not been managing too well since my aunt passed away and he's going to move in with his daughter, my cousin Mary. So there's a spare cottage and in fair condition with a living room, two bedrooms and a big attic for the nets to dry in."

"Are you wanting it for yourself?" Alice asked, unsure of where he lived.

"No, I'm happy enough in my grandfather's old place. I've got plans for it. I was thinking of Ed and Emily and how they could move around the point to Dungeness, now they are wed."

"Tom... Mr Barton, that's a wonderful idea! Emily will be thrilled, I don't think she's ever settled back in Denge. I believe she's forever visiting Connie Webb."

"So perhaps you'll come and let them know. We've two hours until sunset; plenty of time to be there and back."

"I'd love to," Alice replied. "I'll be with you in a few minutes, if you don't mind waiting."

She rushed through the school, full of apologies to Hazel and Ruth, asking them to tidy up

212

and saying she would be out for a while. Then into her bedroom, anxious to be rid of the formal black dress, she pulled on a soft tweed skirt then a pretty blouse and cardigan. The dress was thrown on her bed, with no regard to possible creases. Back through to the kitchen, Alice wrapped chunks of fruit cake; she was hungry after a day's teaching. Snatching a coat from a hook, she ran back through the school, ignoring the surprised glances from her young assistants.

"Tell me about the house, whereabouts is it?" Alice began, having offered Tom a piece of cake.

"It's just past mine, towards the Pilot," Tom replied. "It could do with a few repairs on the seaward side, but that's to be expected. It's a nice place though. Comes with most of the furniture and I know he got a decent range a few years back."

"A range. Emily will be thrilled!" Alice could see the open fire in the Denge shack and whatever had been done to make the home better, a smoking fire spoiled everything.

They walked on in silence for a while after that, taking a route straight across the ridges, keeping the lighthouse to their left. Alice struggled at times and often carried her back-stays, preferring to trudge over the shingle in her walking boots. Tom slowed his pace or let her take the lead.

The sea sparkled a deep blue and a couple of ships could be seen in the distance. A light breeze encouraged cotton wool clouds to scurry across the sky forming and reforming shapes as they went. The air was fresh and slightly salty.

Alice had been deep in thought about Ed and Emily Brooks and the changes in their lives; finally she voiced some of her thoughts:

"Will Ed move, do you think? He is a proud man and loves his home."

"For all his mistakes and a bit of a temper, he'll see sense over this, I'm sure," Tom replied. "I've plans to get him on the lifeboat crew."

"A chance to make amends," Alice reflected.

"There's only Ed's parents and Emily's mother left at Denge," Tom paused and offered a hand to help Alice up a shingle ridge. She paused, uncertain, then accepted it for a moment, letting go as soon as she was steady.

Silence hung between them as they both knew why the population of Denge had halved overnight. With Jake Brooks gone, his widow had no choice but to move further along the coast to Camber, knowing that she could neither support herself and her three children at Denge nor expect Ed to bear the burden.

"They'll still be close enough that Emily can check on them daily." Tom was now thinking of the family left behind, "They could all move in together, but I was hoping to improve their home, not make it more crowded. I imagine the old folk will want to stay at Denge, I just hope they won't stand in the way of this move."

"I'm sure Ed and Emily will do what's right and there are others here who can help out," Alice replied.

As they neared Denge, Alice could see there had been some changes. Something was different but at first she couldn't quite place what had changed. Ed appeared from behind his home and gave them a wave.

"I've been making repairs to my parents' place," he said, "It got the worst of the storm last week."

Then Alice realised, "One of the cottages has gone."

"It was in a bad way, so my Pa, he's been taking it down all week and we can make repairs to the others."

Emily appeared, having heard voices and her face was all smiles on seeing Tom and Alice.

"I'm glad to have found you both, we've got some news." Tom began. "I'll get straight to it – there's an empty property round the point and I thought it might suit you."

"What for us really?" Emily turned to look at Ed, "Can we? Can we move round the point?"

"Just hold back a minute," Ed replied. "Come on in and we'll have a cup o' tea and a chat about it. I'm not saying 'no', Em, I'm just saying that we need to hear more about it."

"Of course you do," Tom said, "and a cup of tea would be welcome, thank you."

The kettle was boiling in no time and Emily had a tin of drop scones full of plump sultanas which she placed on the table. Alice noticed the shack was a lot fresher now the nets had been moved, although the smell of wood smoke was still strong. A small settee sat below the window where the nets had been, giving a more homely look to the room.

They all sat at the table, which now had four matching chairs. "We got these chairs from Ida's," Emily informed.

"It's certainly looking smarter in here," Tom said.

"Thanks to Miss Tibbs," Ed replied.

Alice glanced at Tom and in the exchange of looks they both knew that the other was remembering. It was never spoken about. Alice wondered if the two men ever mentioned it amongst themselves; she thought not. Their secret lay buried in a shallow shingle grave. Ed and Emily's tidier new home had come at higher price than they could imagine, the life of his cousin. But, that wasn't fair, Alice reminded herself. He (she couldn't even think his name) had done wrong and what followed was an accident, a terrible accident and he had paid the price of attempting to assault her.

Alice brushed the thoughts away; she would not be plagued by them. "Tell them about about the cottage, Mr Barton. I don't think Emily can wait until the tea is brewed."

"Well, it's a smart little place, my uncle lives there but he's getting no younger so he's moving in with my cousin, Mary. It could do with a few repairs, they always do being on the coast, but nothing you can't fix during the summer. It's along by the Pilot, not far from my place and only five minutes or so from the Webbs' cottage.

"And it's all right is it? All right with your uncle?" Ed asked.

"I've had a word and there's no one else that needs it. I've got my Granddad's place and his Mary, she's all set up now and her sister, she moved to Lydd. It's yours if you want it. If you want the furniture and the range you can come to an agreement, pay him a bit every month until it's settled."

"What do you think Ed?" Emily's eyes shone as she looked up at him, sitting beside her.

"It all sounds fair enough. We could do with a bit more space and to move the boat around the point would be mean the lads who help me wouldn't have to walk around The Point every day."

"How many rooms does it have?" Emily asked.

"There's the kitchen-cum-living room, about the same size as this and then two bedrooms, both a good size. Out the back, there's the water closet and a shed. My cousin, Mary, she has a copper and wash-house by hers and they all share it, the four houses." Tom paused, "And the loft, it's got a fair sized loft with a ladder going up the outside to it, you know what I mean. Plenty of space for your nets."

"Thank you very much, we appreciate it and I can't say no to providing Emily with a better home. And to bring the boat to Dungeness, well, that will make life easier." Ed took a sip of his tea and continued, "Best we come and have a look at it, if that's all right with your uncle."

"He'll be fine with that," Tom replied. "We'll be back on the two o'clock tide on Sunday, so say half-past four. Does that suit you?"

"Perfect," replied Emily. "I'll be that excited, I don't know how I'll think of anything else until I see it."

"That all sounds fair enough," Ed agreed

"Will you be able to come and look with us, Miss Tibbs?" Emily asked. "It needs another woman to see what needs doing."

"Emily, I'd very much like to but I'm going back to Ashford on the ten-fifteen."

"Of course, back home for Easter. It sounds funny saying that," Emily paused for a moment to reflect on her words. "I mean to say that I forget that you have a home back in Ashford. I always think that you belong here, don't you think so Tom?"

Alice was kept from hearing Tom's opinion on the matter and he was given a reprieve from having to voice it as it was Ed who replied to his wife: "Miss Tibbs has her young man back home in Ashford and a wedding in the summer."

"How silly, excuse my bad manners Miss Tibbs, I thought... I mean to say..." No one knew what Emily

217

thought because she changed the subject, "More tea, Mr Barton... Tom?"

The sun was setting towards Rye as Alice and Tom walked back from Denge. It added a warmth to the grey shingle and made the sea a richer shade of blue. It was wonderful to be a part of improving someone's life and Alice felt a glow of contentment. As they reached the lighthouse, they paused before going their own way home, Tom along the coast towards the Pilot and Alice along the tracks to the schoolhouse.

"You'll be going home for Easter on Saturday," he said. "Two weeks back in Ashford, there will be blossom on the trees and daffodils in the gardens."

"Yes, I imagine there will be," Alice replied. "How odd, I hadn't really thought of it recently, how different it is here I mean."

"Perhaps you've got used to it."

"Perhaps I have, but it will be lovely to see the blossom on a tree and the spring bulbs, Mother has such a pretty display of tulips." Alice looked around at the shingle ground with its tough grass and tenacious little plants.

"Dungeness has a beauty of its own and in the summer we'll have our own little flowers, but perhaps you'll have to look harder for them, they'll be more subtle."

"I'll have plenty of time before I return in July, and what of the broom and gorse, will that will flower by July?"

"Yes, that will be in flower when you return and be bold enough. You'll see a bit of colour by late spring. Then you'll go back to the town to be married and be that busy you'll forget all about us."

"Oh no," Alice looked up at him, "I wouldn't do that and I'll visit, of course I'll visit."

"Visiting isn't the same," he replied. "You're not part of it any more."

"No, I don't suppose I will be."

"Time to move on," Tom said.

"Time to move on," Alice repeated thoughtfully.

Chapter Twenty-Three

Alice left Dungeness for Ashford on the following Saturday. As the wheels of the tank engine gathered pace, the light rains falling from low clouds were left behind, hanging over the shingle headland. She passed through Lydd and, as the train reached Appledore, the sky was blue with white wisps of cloud. From the grimy window, Alice looked out to appreciate the lush green fields and occasional group of playful lambs.

Soon she was nearing Ashford and the parish church with its pinnacled tower could be seen; a cluster of Tudor, Georgian and Victorian buildings nestled around it. Set before the town, Alice could see Ashford's railway station and works, and to the right, her future home in Newtown. The engine eased onto one of four tracks between the two platforms. Alice scanned the area under the deep, ornate canopies and soon spotted her parents who were, just as eagerly, looking for their daughter.

By the time the engine came to a halt, Alice was already on her feet, holding onto her seat to steady herself. Then, hauling her suitcase through the carriage doorway, where it was taken by Reverend Tibbs.

"Alice, it's been so long. All through this dreadful winter. Let me look at you." Her mother released Alice from her embrace and looked into her face. "I shall have to get used to your fringe, even though I saw it at Christmas. You look a little older; it must be teaching all those children. You mustn't forget to cream your face at night."

"My dear, she must become older. Do not fuss so." Reverend Tibbs gave his daughter an affectionate pat on the arm. "Splendid to see you, my dear, we can't wait to hear all your news."

A porter hovered and was charged with the duty of carrying Alice's case to the pony and trap waiting patiently outside the station yard. They walked along the platform and out through the station building and all the time Alice felt quite dazed by it all. Where was the fresh country air that Ashford boasted? Here it was all smoke and steam, laced with pipe tobacco. So many people, the staff, those who had just come off the train and those about to join the train. They called to each other in unfamiliar accents for the coming of the railway had brought workers from all over the country.

Outside the station, the railway omnibus was preparing to take travellers to town. For Alice, it was a ride in the trap to the peace and quiet of the Willesborough Rectory. They turned towards the town jostling for a place on the busy road between town and station. Men in cloth caps, astride push bikes, weaved their way around the carts. A familiar Lion Brewery horse-drawn van passed them at a fair speed, causing the Reverend to mutter ungodly words under his breath and for Alice to feel quite nervous at the pace of life back home in Ashford.

Thankfully, they skirted the town centre and the long road out to Willesborough was more peaceful. As the white, weather-boarded Sprotlands windmill neared, the pony instinctively turned into Church

221

Road. There was the spire of her father's church, St Mary the Virgin, and finally they turned into the Rectory.

As before, Albert was to come for afternoon tea. Now spring was here, Alice was hoping that he would agree to stroll over to Newtown. He was sure to know which house was to be theirs and they could have a look at the outside. Perhaps during the week, Alice and her mother could even go and introduce themselves to the current tenant and have a look inside.

There was a rap on the door and there he was looking just the same as always… but perhaps his hair was a little shorter, or maybe just slicked down more neatly.

"Alice dearest, at last you are with us again," Albert held both her hands and looked into her face. "Home at last. How I have worried about you and the wisdom of you being so far from home."

"I am fine, Albert. I'm sure this time away before we marry has been an adventure I can always look back on."

"Nevertheless, perhaps a position closer to home would have been wiser."

Stepping through into the dining room, Albert's attention was fully on her parents as they all went through the familiar motions of enquiries about work, family and comments on recent news. Alice became more and more desperate to have word of her future home. It seemed that every minute lasted an age but she must just sit and wait for a moment of silence in order to ask about what must surely be the most interesting topic for them all. Finally it was the Reverend who asked the all-important question:

"What news do you have on the house, Albert?

Has this Mr Baldwin set a retirement date yet?"

"Bad news, sir. Bad news indeed." Albert bowed his head slightly to portray the burden of telling. "I was told just this week that Mr Baldwin is to retire at the end of July but his replacement comes from Manchester with a family of five children. His need for a house is greater than ours."

"That is bad luck and after all your hopes and expectations. Very disappointing." The Reverend shook his head in dismay and pushed his sandwiches aside for a moment whilst he reflected on the news.

Alice didn't speak. She had seen it all: she was to see Albert off in the morning from the front door and watch him walk past the trees and across the green; she would walk to the local shop or the library with a shopping basket over her arm; she would watch her husband work on the allotment at the weekend. Alice had seen her life centred in a terraced house set on the green with the noise and bustle of the railway works in the background. What was she to picture now?

Her mother was talking, Alice had heard the words but couldn't recall them. She forced herself to listen.

"...Might there be another opportunity? You deserve a house, Albert, they must see that. A good worker must surely have a house when he marries? Do you know of any others? Have you heard of any more being built, for that was the plan; they always intended to build more, you know..."

"There is a chance of a flat, but Mother says and I must agree, that why would we live in a flat when she has a decent house with space for us all?"

So, that was the plan. To live with Albert's mother. A good plan and what most young couples expected. But, Alice couldn't picture it. What would her role be in a place where his mother already had all her routines in place, just as she liked them? Her body felt heavy, crushed by the disappointment.

When Albert left, two hours later, Alice had barely spoken. However, a plan had been made for the two of them to travel by train to Folkestone the next day. The weather looked good and a walk along the Leas with the chance of seeing across the sea to France was appealing. A good walk and some fresh air would surely revive Alice's spirits.

Sitting in her father's church the following evening, Alice reflected that it had been a very pleasant day. It was all she could have hoped for on a day out with her handsome Albert, who was at all times attentive and courteous. But however much she told herself it had been the perfect day, a slight feeling of depression persisted.

Later in the week, Alice and her mother left the Reverend home at his desk preparing the parish newsletter. They strolled into Ashford town, a walk of forty-five minutes along the rural road from Willesborough. Clumps of butter yellow primroses adorned the grass verges and the trees were beginning to display tender green leaves.

"Your father needs some writing paper and envelopes," Mother had said earlier. "And it's Aunt Maud's birthday so I'd like to look in the William Giles store to see if anything takes my fancy. Not forgetting your wedding dress, we'll pick out some material and have Mrs Saunders make it up."

After half an hour they crossed the River Stour and left the farmland behind them. Turning to the left they walked along East Hill with The Star pub, fine

Georgian houses and substantial red brick walls. Soon the tall houses became interspersed with shops as they entered the lower end of the High Street.

Their first stop was Headley's Print and Stationers, midway along the High Street. They stepped under the canopied entrance and into the shop. Alice loved the timeless order of paper, notebooks and envelopes on the dark wooden shelves. She inspected the ink-pens and pencils. This was a shop she had visited many times before with both her parents as it was a favourite of her father's. On the spur of the moment, Alice choose a pen for Hazel. It would be lovely to return with a gift for her friend.

Next, mother and daughter went into William Giles, glass and china store.

"You'll have a home of your own soon enough, Alice," her mother said as she veered towards the sets of crockery. "It's just a case of waiting and in the meantime there is plenty to collect for your bottom drawer. How do you like this Spode Blue Italian pattern."

"I find it rather fussy," Alice replied with disinterest. "I'm not sure I want so much pattern on my dinner plate." She moved towards a different display, "These Wedgwood plates with the mandarin border are nice, or perhaps the etruria. Just a pattern around the edge."

"Too fussy!" repeated Mrs Tibbs. "When I was setting up home, the more decoration the better."

Alice picked up a few more items, casting them back on the shelf without interest. She turned away from the crockery displays. "Did you say a pot-pourri dish for Aunt Maud?"

"You'll have to decide on these things soon you

know, Alice." Mrs Tibbs walked briskly towards the cut glass ornaments display.

On leaving the shop, Mrs Tibbs made a bee-line for her favourite material shop which was in one of the timber framed Tudor buildings nestling under the shadow of the church. Her mind still on Alice's bottom drawer she headed towards the linens.

"French or Irish?" the enthusiastic mother asked her daughter.

"I... I... really don't mind," Alice replied.

Mrs Tibbs inspected some bales of material then instructed the assistant to cut off several meters of a French cotton with a high thread count. "We'll hem these in the evenings over the next week," she told Alice.

She then descended on the white and ivory silks, taking samples to the natural light at the windows to inspect the colour and quality.

"I wonder," Alice began, "... I wonder if perhaps a mauve or a pale pink... or even... or even a dove grey would be both pretty and more practical? I could use it again... perhaps make a few alterations."

"Well, I don't really think... it's not what I was expecting. Not what I was expecting at all," Mrs Tibbs looked straight at Alice. "Let's look at the pattern books."

"Not too fussy, please Mother."

"Fussy! That word again. When did a bride not want a fuss on her wedding?"

Mother and daughter left the shop with a book of patterns to borrow and small samples of both ivory and a rose pink. The cotton was to be delivered to their home by the end of the day.

"Now for something to eat," Mrs Tibbs announced and strode off leaving Alice to trail behind.

It was the afternoon of Easter Monday; Alice had been invited to have afternoon tea with Albert and his mother. Albert called for her and they walked around the corner to his home. He lived, with his mother, in a modern, orange brick semi-detached house with a pretty bay window. His mother was fond of flowers and spent many hours a week tending the garden. As soon as a bloom was past its best, its head was snipped off, and no new growth was allowed to go untended as it was either cut into shape or trained into place. As Alice stepped up the garden path she appreciated the tulips, daffodils and grape hyacinth. Around the front door the wisteria was yet to bloom for a couple of months.

Alice had never been further than the front parlour, which was reserved for Sundays and guests. How very strange that it seemed unlikely she would see any other part of the house until it became her home. She sat on a mahogany chair at the small table which stood in the bay window and surveyed the room. After tea, she would sit on the settee at Albert's side whilst his mother relaxed in the armchair

It was a pleasant place in which to sit and look out over the street. A writing slope was placed on a bookcase and Alice imagined that Mrs Havers often lifted the slope onto the table and sat there writing her letters. The table was covered with a dark red cloth and then a lace over-cloth. Curtains and a scalloped edge pelmet were also a dark red, this time in velvet. The fireplace, with its pretty tiles, had a small fire in its grate. Walls, papered in a dark gold paisley pattern, were embellished with needlework pictures and decorative plates. The fireplace and bookcase were adorned with figurines, vases and a fine carriage clock.

It was a fine, decorative room which Mrs

Havers kept in good order. Alice could see this would be a pleasant home for her, but couldn't shift the slight feeling of depression settling upon her. How often would all those dainty ornaments need dusting, she wondered, and what would she have to write about when sitting at this very table as the new Mrs Havers?

"Alice dear, I had a notion that you and I could work on a cross stitch together, to celebrate your wedding." Mrs Havers suggested as she poured the tea.

"That's a lovely idea," Alice replied. It really was very thoughtful of Albert's mother. "Perhaps we could walk to town in the week and choose the threads?"

"I'd like that very much," Mrs Havers smiled warmly at Alice. "I never had a daughter and I so look forward to spending time with you. When we are finished, Albert could frame it. He has quite a collection of woodworking tools in his shed now."

"A fair collection," Albert agreed.

The three of them continued to nibble on dainty sandwiches, scones and ginger cake. It was all very pleasant and Alice thought she would enjoy learning to cook under the guidance of her new mother-in-law. But what else would she do beside the dusting, shopping and washing her delicate clothes? Most of the laundry was done by a local woman and a daily help did the sweeping and mopping. Would she help in the garden or might she be able to work few days a week? Alice broached the subject with Albert when his mother left them alone after tea.

"Albert, of course I want to do my share of chores and help your mother wherever I can, but there are only three of us with a daily help. Now we are not to have our own home perhaps I could help your mother and work as well?"

"Alice, bless you for wanting to educate young minds, but you see how Mother is looking forward to having your company, so we cannot deprive her." Albert patted Alice's arm tenderly.

"I just feel that I would like to do something useful," Alice persisted weakly.

"And so you will," Albert held her gaze with his own blue eyes. "You will be marvellous company for mother and perhaps the two of you could do something beneficial to the community, such as helping the local people who are elderly or infirm. I am sure your father, the Reverend, would know of families who would greatly benefit from having their shopping done for them or some company during the day."

"I'm sure he would," Alice agreed. "I need to feel useful."

"I was talking to Mother only this morning and we wondered about the wisdom of you returning to your teaching position. We no longer need your income to furnish our own home and Mother gets so lonely, you could be here, visiting daily and getting to know each other."

"Oh, I hadn't... I mean to say that..." Alice couldn't express her thoughts coherently. Not to go back to Dungeness that she had at first, she was ashamed to admit, sneered upon and hated for its chilled sea mists and dreary grey landscape, when now it had become a part of her. She had seen beauty did not have to be apple blossom and oak trees. Yes, they were all very fine, but beauty came in different forms. The subtle grey tones of shingle ridges and the grey-blue of a stormy sky had their own wild appeal.

Albert sat looking down at her, as someone might look at a pretty kitten or newly-born lamb. "Of

229

course my darling, you are thinking of your commitment to the school and pupils and I admire you for it. However, your greater loyalty is towards your family... your future family."

"Yes, I see," Alice replied.

"I am not saying a letter would suffice, no if you were to go to see Mrs Stubbs then that would show good manners and I am sure she will understand. She sounds like an eminently sensible woman. Yes, that it the thing to do."

"Yes, I imagine it would be," Alice agreed.

"Mother will be delighted and now we can look forward to Sunday afternoon walks or day trips all through the spring and summer." Albert's blue eyes shone and with his smartly slicked dark brown hair he looked so handsome gazing down at her. He lifted her hands to his lips, "Oh my love, how happy you make me."

Chapter Twenty-Four

"Lydd, Lydd. All alight for Lydd. Next stop Dungeness."
The station master called out with all the importance
he could muster. It may only be Lydd, but to him it was
just as important as Paddington or Charing Cross.

Alice looked out through the grimy window at
the smart little station. Containers of spring flowers sat
against the warm orange brick of the long, low
buildings with their slate clad roofs. A scallop edged
canopy shaded the doorway and to either side was a
row of arched sash windows. It was a fine building,
lacking the worldly Italianate influences of Ashford
Station, but rather pleasant for a country station.

She was alone in the one coach that was all
the Lydd Railway Company deemed necessary to
transport the people of this remote corner of Kent.
However, on this bright, albeit breezy, April afternoon,
Alice was sure to be joined by housewives who had
travelled to Lydd for provisions and would now be
returning to Dungeness. Eagerly she scanned the
platform as best she could, given the build-up of soot
on the windows, and was disappointed to only see the
station master and his assistant.

It seemed that no one was going to accompany
her on this last leg of the journey; it was to be just
Alice. The coach doors had been slammed shut, the
whistle blown and the flag waved when the integrity of
the guard and all the rules he stood for were

compromised by a latecomer. A shout alerted the guard, who could not bring himself to assist this person who disrespected the Lydd Railway Company timetable, and merely bristled with annoyance. The young man flung himself at the door of the coach, turning the handle and opening the door as the engine made those first slow turns of its great wheels. Belches of steam were being released through the chimney as he staggered into the coach.

"Well, I just saved myself a long walk in this damned wind." His voice was cheerful but rough and, as he spoke, he flung himself down in the set of seats across the aisle from Alice and placed a bag beside him. Dark blonde curls were a little untidy, with no hat to keep them in place. He was freshly shaved though, sideburns neatly shaped. Grey eyes looked towards Alice and soft lines around them crinkled slightly as he smiled. His trousers and waistcoat were clean and of a decent fit, Alice observed. Not overly smart, but he was a fisherman and had no need to dress up like a city gent.

"Miss Tibbs, how did you enjoy your Easter holidays? I trust all was fine in Ashford; perhaps the weather was a little warmer?"

"The weather was fair, thank you, and as always it was good to see my family." Alice smiled back at the person who had irritated her so much on her arrival at Dungeness last autumn. He may be very different from the few men of her previous acquaintance, but her mind was broader now and she knew him to be a hard-working, respected member of the community here.

"Ed and Emily are happily settled now," Tom remarked. "She's so much happier and he's on the lifeboats now."

232

"Do people accept him... forgive him?"

"Mostly they do, those that know him and see him for a decent fellow. He's a good sort, always willing to help others and grateful for the help we've given him."

"I'm glad to hear it. He's a hard worker, and Emily too."

For a moment, Alice reflected on another time, on another journey from Ashford to Dungeness. It seemed like a lifetime ago, when she had arrived in the relentless wind and rain, only to stumble over the body of Emily Brooks. How lacking in life experience she had been and how fixed in her opinions. It seemed that the Alice who arrived six months ago was a different person, and in many ways she was.

The steam train passed the school and Alice looked over, hoping Hazel would be there when she arrived. She had missed the friendship of another young woman, having only her parents and Albert for company whilst she was at home. Hazel had decided to return to her family while Alice was away; she found it lonely being in the schoolhouse and away from the other cottages.

"Your last term then," Tom stated. "Then back to Ashford with memories of the summer sun shining down on you."

"Oh, I don't think the sea mist and wind are that easily forgotten," Alice smiled. "Actually it's not my last term though... I've written to Mrs Stubbs and I am to stay on after the summer. In fact I'll probably stay here for the summer and just visit my family in Ashford from time to time."

"And your... your marriage?"

"I think I've changed... I'm not his type of woman anymore," She paused, her cheeks colouring a little, and looked down at her hands and the indent showing where her engagement ring had been, "Neither do I believe that Albert would suit me."

Her companion didn't reply to this, perhaps unsure of how to respond. Commiserating with a young woman on the end of her engagement was beyond his sphere of experience. So they sat in silence for a moment, intent on looking out of the windows. The train slowed as it approached the station and gave a final shudder as it came to a halt.

Tom stood up as the train came to a stop. Without a word he reached for Alice's heavy suitcase, made his way to the door and opened it. Stepping out he placed the case on the platform and held the door open for her.

"Thank you." She looked up at him and went to place her hand on the case.

"I'll carry it to the schoolhouse for you," Tom said, his own hand reaching the handle before hers. "It's very heavy."

They set off across the shingle, both still absorbed with their own thoughts. For Alice, she saw the place afresh, as somewhere she would settle, for the time being at least. She looked with new eyes at the variation in the tones of the grey-brown stones and at the fragile plants that were raising their heads now the sun was shining.

Rough grasses had an unusual rusty-red tinge to them as their seed-heads ripened, making an attractive carpet stretching in all directions. Pretty white flowers on grey-green stems risked reaching out to the sun on the desolate shingle-land. Now, in contrast to the subtle hues, the gorse was beginning to display its vibrant yellow flowers. Alice found herself pausing to look closer at a delicate seed-head or to marvel at the brilliant blue spikes of viper's bugloss. Tulips and daffodils were all very pleasant, but here was different form of beauty and it was just as engaging.

The companions passed a few comments occasionally, on safe subjects such as the weather or a distinctive sea-bird that flew past. Tom named some of the plants which Alice had stooped to examine. Alice apologised for taking her time and that the suitcase was so heavy.

At the schoolhouse door, Tom placed the case down. "It's nice over Littlestone way, with tall houses overlooking the bay... and a decent path along the seafront," he began tentatively at first and paused before continuing, "...and a fine hotel where they do a nice afternoon tea, so I hear. The train goes there from Lydd and it's a pleasant stroll to the promenade."

Alice looked up at him and waited.

"So I wondered Alice... if perhaps next Saturday...?"

"That would be lovely," Alice replied.

"Good. Well, have a good week then and I'll see you... I'll knock for you at ten o'clock next Saturday."

"I'll look forward to it."

Tom turned away. After a few steps he paused to wave, as he closed the gate in the picket fence behind him. Then, with a grin on his face, he set off towards his wooden seaside home.

THE END

About the Author

Emma Batten loves to combine her interest in local history with creative writing. She has this to say about where she lives on Romney Marsh:

Romney Marsh is a fascinating place. Once under the sea, it has evolved over the last two centuries to be the low-lying land we see today. The countryside can be bleak, but reed-lined drainage ditches and red-berried hawthorn have their own special beauty. The seaside villages can easily be dismissed if you look no further than the arcades and ice-cream shops, but they have a colourful history. And then there is the shingle spit at Dungeness: a truly unique landscape favoured by artists, film-makers and writers. What about the people who used to live there? We can only imagine what their lives were like.

Emma is keen to work with local artists and cover designers. She loves 'meet the author' events and selling books locally, enabling her to meet the people who read her books. She offers two talks: The Journey of a Self-Published Author and The History of Romney Marsh as Seen Through my Novels.

The Books

A Place Called Hope is Emma's first novel. It tells the story of young women living in a tiny settlement named Hope, which was near New Romney.

Secrets of the Shingle, is her second novel.

What The Monk Didn't See is Emma's third Romney Marsh novel. It tells the story of the 1287 storm, which changed the fortunes of New Romney forever.

Her fourth, *But First Maintain the Wall,* is set in 18th century Dymchurch and tells the story of the people who lived in the shadows of the vast seawall.

Her fifth, *Stranger on The Point,* is a sequel to *Secrets of the Shingle* and follows the story of Lily, who struggles to fulfil her worth as the shadows of the First World War live on. Set in Dungeness, Lydd and Ashford

The Artist's Gift is Emma's sixth novel, and is a sequel to *Stranger on the Point.* Beginning with the bombing of Lydd Church in 1941, it follows real wartime events as seen through the eyes of fictional characters.

www.emmabattenauthor.com